WORST NEIGHBOR EVER

A SWORN TO LOATHE YOU PREQUEL

RACHEL JOHN

ACKNOWLEDGMENTS

Can you dedicate a book to an idea? I really wanted a fake Witness Protection fiancé in a story. And a wild Granny. And I kept trying to come up with a more normal plotline, but this one was like, no. It's happening. So, it did.

CHAPTER 1

←——————————————→

MELISSA

I should have seen it coming. It was the day before my twenty-ninth birthday, and Mom unexpectedly wanted to meet up and go shoe shopping.

I had told her I didn't need shoes, but she doubled down, saying that was even better. We could focus on finding her the perfect pair of summer sandals, and I wouldn't be distracted with trying on anything for myself.

My mother could talk a comedian out of their last joke. She's just that good.

So we went shoe shopping, bra shopping, and furniture browsing until the commissioned sales people there gave up and wished us dead, and just when I thought she might let me go home and waste the rest of my Saturday on my own terms, she announced she needed to use the bathroom.

My mother does not do public restrooms. She's developed an iron bladder to cope, but sometimes when you gotta go, you gotta go. And my house was closer.

I had just bought one side of a duplex in a cute neighborhood where all the lawns were green and mowed, except for ours, and I was totally going to remedy the situation whether my deadbeat duplex neighbor ever decided to help or not. He'd been avoiding meeting me, probably because of the yard situation, and perhaps because he had something sketchy going on over there with all the cars coming and going at all hours.

As I pulled up to my new house, the expanse of dull brown against the green of the other yards had me wrinkling my nose. Mom jumped out the passenger-side door the second I stopped at the curb. I tossed her the keys, and she ran inside like she was about to win the fifty-yard dash.

After turning into my carport and enjoying the quiet for a moment, I gathered up my shopping bags and went around to the front door. In her haste, Mom had left the keys in the lock. I pulled them out and tucked them in the front pocket of my jeans.

Today hadn't been so bad. I had a new pair of cute sandals and a new black lace bra that managed to give me a nice lift without digging into my sides. I hadn't wanted to try it on at all, but after Mom announced to everyone in Macy's that my once-white bras were gray and not quite getting the job done anymore, heading into the dressing room suddenly sounded like a great idea.

I turned my door handle, preparing to deposit my bags on the end table, and instead dropped them on the floor as a dozen voices yelled, "Surprise!"

I blinked, trying to make my eyes adjust to so many people with their expectant gazes on me, most of them practically strangers. Neighbors, I quickly realized. Ones I had only waved to once or twice, but who now had been forced in here by my formidable mother in her attempt to make me new friends. It was seventh grade all over again. Oh crap, I was beginning to sweat. I mentally backtracked to this morning to make sure I'd put on deodorant. Check. Check. My panic subsided a smidge.

"Happy Birthday!" several people said at once.

My across-the-street neighbor pushed her way toward me just as everyone began singing the birthday song with off-key enthusiasm. "Hi, sorry." She leaned closer so she could whisper-yell above the singing. "Your mom said to gather everyone at four, put up the banner, and wait in here. I'm sorry. I should have told her—"

"No, it's fine." It wasn't this woman's job to go toe-to-toe with my mother. I was just relieved someone else got how weird this was. "But um, how did you get in here?"

"She told me where you keep your extra key hidden, so you may want to move that, but um, first..." She gave me a subtle head tilt down. "Let's take care of your shopping bags." It was then I realized my brand-new bra with its very supportive cups and optional padding was nestled between our feet. She'd probably kicked it back toward me on her way over. I couldn't remember her name for the life of me, but that didn't matter. We were officially kindred spirits. I reached down to pick up the bra, but the strap was under her shoe.

She took a step back, but that only created a stretchy tug-o-war between my hand and her foot. By the time I had the thing safely back in the bag, I'm pretty sure every person there could identify it in a line-up if they had to, and my poor neighbor had apologized four more times. I had to start looking like I was having a good time or the awkwardness levels in here were going to kill us all.

"It was a successful shopping trip," I said to no one in particular. I couldn't bear to make eye contact with anyone until my face didn't feel like the surface of the sun. I liked meeting people, but this? This was all the things I hated wrapped up in one—surprises, sudden loud noises, unexpected guests, and forced obligation. I was obligated to make this party a success because it was mine. You couldn't be the pooper of your own party.

After a deep breath, I went around shaking hands and introducing myself, which was super embarrassing, since birthday parties were supposed to be filled with the people who knew and loved you. All the people who fit in those categories were taking me out to dinner tomorrow night. My dad wasn't even here. He was probably out giving golf lessons and had no idea what Mom was up to. She was a stealthy one with her shenanigans. If she'd told any of my friends or family about this surprise party, there would have been no party, and no surprise.

Speaking of people who loved me, where were my dogs? They would have been all over me the instant I came in the door, and despite the major distraction that was this party, I felt guilty for forgetting them, even for a minute.

"Mom." I took her aside, giving the neighbor she was talking to an apologetic smile. "Where are Buster and Sarge?" I didn't have a fence up outside yet. I was terrified she'd sent them out back, and they might be roaming the neighborhood looking for trouble.

"Natalya has them. I told her I was cleaning your house from top to bottom as a birthday surprise. She's coming back with them soon. Don't fret."

That made me feel a little better, despite finding out my mother's lies in planning this party were a cavern I'd probably never see the bottom of. At least my dogs were in good hands. They were probably living it up at Natalya's house.

"Time for cake," my mom called out, rallying the group towards my kitchen, where a banner hung with the words, 'Forever 29!' I bet my mom did a Google search for birthday banners, not realizing this one was for women who had long

4

past that age. Hilarious. When she wasn't driving me crazy, my mom was unintentionally hilarious.

I wondered who had been roped into bringing the cake. Maybe my mom bought it for them and made them store it in their fridge along with a promise to come. Ack, it was probably better not to know.

I forced myself to smile at the few stragglers still standing with me in the living room, but then I caught sight of the guy sitting casually in my armchair in the corner. I couldn't smile at that. At *him*.

He was reading a manuscript on pink scented paper, deeply engrossed, with an amused and slightly smug smile on his face. He looked up at me and then TURNED THE PAGE. No shame whatsoever that he was a snoop—a smug snoop, and a bad neighbor, and a tree and grass killer. Oh, and probably a criminal who sold shady goods out of his house. I couldn't forget that little detail. The fact that I found him to be the handsomest guy I'd ever laid eyes on only made me more irritated. Who did he think he was, sitting there leafing through my stuff? Yeah, no more having an emergency key out. In fact, I should probably change my locks, just in case.

"Hey, neighbor," he said when I marched over and held out my hand, palm up.

"Reading time is over."

He sighed and closed the pink manuscript before turning his beautiful blue-green eyes on me. They were like a sun-sparkled lakeshore. An evil lakeshore, I amended. Probably one infested with piranhas.

"Did you write this?" he asked, lifting it up to his nose to give the papers a sniff. "And is that cinnamon I detect?"

"Potpourri. And no, I didn't write it."

"What's potpourri?"

"Let's just put it on the list of stuff that's not your concern." I wiggled the fingers of my outstretched hand, but as I expected, he didn't hand the manuscript back. He knew I wanted it, and that was reason enough to be a tease about it. I had just failed the most basic rule of power struggles—the most emotional person in the argument is always the loser.

I took a deep breath. "Sorry, it's just been a very long day, and now I have twenty strangers in my house. Not that you'd care. You have strangers in and out of your house all the time, am I right?"

"I'm Connor." He reached out his hand for me to shake, completely ignoring my little dig, and also not returning the manuscript, which was tucked securely under his other arm.

I frowned at his outstretched hand. "I'm not shaking your hand. You're leaving."

I expected him to balk, but he stood and handed me the manuscript. "Happy Birthday, Melissa. Sorry I offended you. This is actually pretty good. You should get it published."

"I didn't write it. My granny wrote it. Sort of."

"She sort of wrote it?"

"No. She's sort of my granny. Never mind. Bye, now."

My heart gave a little squeeze as he walked past me, accepting my dismissal with no fight. I'd kind of liked our back and forth, but now that it was one-sided, I just felt mean. He'd complimented me and told me happy birthday, and I'd tossed him out. I didn't like being mean, even to a possible criminal. My bad day wasn't his fault. Mostly.

Connor stopped at the front door and stepped back suddenly when it opened. My dogs charged inside, followed by Natalya, who still looked like a living Barbie doll despite being windblown and overheated. Every May, Phoenix turned into an oven on broil, and every May it took us all by surprise.

Buster and Sarge came right for me, and I immediately commanded them to sit, which they did, reluctantly. Sarge's big tail thumped against the wooden floor, and Buster's wiggly little body turned in three circles before he finally settled.

All the kids in the room came to give the dogs hugs, but despite all that, my attention went back to the doorway where Natalya and Connor were staring each other down, surprise written all over their faces. There was History there, with a capital H, and I needed the details.

"Connor?" Natalya spat out. "What are you doing here? What are all these people doing here?"

"Surprise neighborhood birthday party. They're all the rage now. How are you, Nat? Long time no see."

Her eyes narrowed. "I'm fine. No thanks to you, jerk."

He glanced back at me as I cautiously approached. "You two aren't roommates, are you?" he asked, as if that might be the worst possibility in the world.

Natalya's jaw dropped. "Excuse me?" She looked mad enough to move in with me immediately just to tick him off. And while I loved Natalya, she was better in smaller doses, like Red Vine licorice. Ten pieces or so was divine. Eating a whole bucket? Not recommended.

"Natalya's my best friend, but she doesn't live here. How do you two know each other?"

"We dated," Connor said, a little bit of guilt coating his words. Interesting. It must have been more than two years ago, because that's how long Natalya and I had been friends, and I would have remembered him.

It made sense that they would've dated. One fair-haired and petite except where it counted, and the other tall, dark, and handsome, with exceptionally beautiful eyes. What a couple they made.

Around the room, neighbors of ours were watching the conversation play out with way more interest than was probably good for any of us, so I opened the door back up and Connor quickly slipped out and jogged down the porch steps. Natalya and I followed after I closed the door firmly behind us.

"He ghosted me," Natalya said to me, before turning to Connor and pointing at his retreating back. "And you might not have anything to say for yourself, Connor Harwood, but I'll tell you this. Stay away from Melissa. She's been through enough with her fiancé."

Oh no. Not this. I tried to wave Natalya off at the pass, but she took courage when Connor turned around to face us, looking curious.

"Melissa's fiancé is in the witness protection program. So, she might look single but she's not. She'll never be single."

I'd never be single? I mentally smacked my forehead and pulled Natalya back towards the party. There were dozens of strangers she hadn't embarrassed me in front of yet, and even if my next-door neighbor was a jerk and a girlfriend-ghoster, I felt a new level of mortification at her words I couldn't quite define or understand.

CHAPTER 2

CONNOR

Today I had ignored every instinct that usually kept my life drama free. I didn't have time for drama. I had dental school finals to study for, and a closet full of junk to sell so I could pay my mortgage, and neither of those tasks had anything to do with my neighbor—my beautiful, unconventional neighbor who happened to be best friends with a maniac, and had a trouble-making, albeit well-meaning mother.

I know everyone believes it's women who jump ahead in their thinking to marriage the second they meet someone, but women don't have the exclusive right to that sort of obsessive thinking.

Guys do it, too. Right when they meet a girl's overbearing mother and slowly back away. Or maybe it's just me. I worry about the type of mom I'd like my future children to have because my mother walked out on us when I was ten. My step-mom has been amazing and loving—the perfect example of providing roots and wings. My younger brother gives her a hard time because he doesn't remember the difference. I do. There is a huge difference between emotionally checked out and someone who's *there* for you.

But the fact that I was thinking about all of this instead of studying is exactly why I should've said no the second Mrs. Cooke asked if I'd come to her daughter's surprise birthday party. I should have said no for a lot of reasons.

1. Last week, I hid in my house studying while Melissa's family helped her move in, knowing if I went outside, I'd get roped into moving couches and making conversation. My exams have been social-life killers in every way possible.

2. Melissa didn't know I purposely avoided helping her move in, and I'd like to keep it that way. She also didn't know I was totally checking her out through the blinds before forcing myself back to my test questions. For the record, she's very fine.

3. This one I had no way of predicting, but I couldn't let Natalya Peabody (aka Melissa's best friend) back in my life under any circumstances. It took a lot of work to get her out the first time. I wasn't sure if she'd made up that story about Melissa having a forever fiancé out of pure territorial jealousy, or out of protection from me, but either way, Melissa was off-limits.

4. My roommate, Rob, would love nothing more than to get to know someone like Melissa on a personal level, so the less we all interacted, the better. I told Rob that Melissa was not hot. Thankfully, he hasn't seen her for himself yet.

My phone buzzed and I checked the message from a total stranger. Most of my texts were from total strangers. It was sad, really, when I let myself think about it.

Still have the metal bingo cage for sale?
Yep. $20.
Cool. Txt me your address. I'll be there in 10.

My last roommate before Rob was a major EBay seller (his words) and even though he couldn't afford to pay me the last few months of rent, it was all okay (again, his words) because he'd left me all his crap to sell. Yay for me.

I went to go find the bingo cage and put it on the arm of the couch before returning to studying. Rob would be home any minute, and his new hobby was going to make me lose my mind. I had to find a way to talk him out of the concert thing he wanted to do next weekend.

CHAPTER 3

MELISSA

Like clockwork, I got two letters from Damien in the mail on Monday with no return address. This time, they were postmarked from Louisiana. I wasn't sure how Damien managed to change up the postmarks every time, or why he bothered to go to all that trouble.

Did he think I was so stupid that I still believed he was in the witness protection program? I sighed. Yes, yes he did. The fact that I'd once been that gullible filled me with the same deep embarrassment it always did. His lie was now my lie. Because I'd told people. Because his fiery, yet deeply loyal granny still believed it.

That was why, after coming home from work to feed, love on, and walk Damien's dogs—no, *my* dogs now—I took her letter and drove over to the retirement home where Granny lived. We had three hours before visiting time was over, and she'd want to make the most of it.

Sure enough, Granny was all dressed up and waiting for me in the foyer when I arrived. She had her sunglasses on and a flowery scarf around her head to protect her new hairdo. She never missed Makeover Mondays, and today must have been no exception. With her fire-engine-red lipstick and newly blonde hair, she looked sassier than ever.

I gave the security guard at the front desk a little salute and held open the door for Granny, who was always in a hurry, with only a walker and stiff legs to hold her back from whatever it was she'd set her mind to.

"Did Damien write?" she asked, glancing around as if we might be overheard.

"He did. I'll give you the letter in the car. But right now, we have more important things to deal with."

"Oh." Granny's eyebrows raised, her interest piqued.

Technically, I wasn't even supposed to take Granny out of the retirement home at all, and I'd almost been arrested the first time I did it. They let me go after a long discussion with both the police and the staff of the retirement home. I was her only visitor, and Granny needed adventure, something to look forward to, and family ties. I could provide all those things safely. So, as long as I had her back by eight p.m. nobody bothered us about pesky things like felony endangerment and kidnapping anymore.

I got Granny into the passenger side and folded up her walker, stuffing it into the backseat before getting in on the driver's side.

"What's this about important things?" Granny asked while perusing her letter from Damien. She smiled as she read. He always had such sweet things to say, the louse.

"An anonymous client has asked us to pick up a package for her and deliver it to a home at this address." I put a finger to my lips before handing her a folded piece of paper with an address. "We'll need to make sure we're not followed," I whispered.

Bless Natalya and her willingness to go along with anything I asked, no matter how bizarre. She had prepped the package and left it for us, and if all went as planned, she'd be the mysterious sedan following us from two cars back while we made the delivery.

I'd learned the hard, embarrassing way that it was better to plan out an adventure rather than let Granny interrogate people about unsolved crimes she'd read about in the newspaper. Okay, so I'd almost been arrested *twice*. At least life was never boring with Granny involved. Her grandson, and her son, for that matter, were way missing out.

"I loved your latest romance novel, Granny," I said. "You sure you're not ready to publish?"

"Don't push me on this. I want them published anonymously after I die, and the money goes to charity. That's the deal."

"Of course. It's just, you might have a new fan." I wasn't sure why I wanted to bring up Connor so badly. Maybe it was because he was a mystery I couldn't solve, especially if I was banned from discussing him with the one person qualified to give me information. All Natalya would say was that he deserved to be alone, and I should avoid the man like the plague. I was avoiding him, at least physically. Now if I could just get him out of my thoughts...

"You let people see my manuscript?" Granny frowned at me before going back to checking the mirrors for tails. I probably shouldn't encourage her suspicious nature, but she just enjoyed these adventures so much.

"My new neighbor picked it up and read some. He thought I wrote it."

"The neighbor who doesn't take care of his yard and peered at you through his windows while you moved in? You let that loser into your house?"

I laughed. Okay, maybe I had talked about Connor before. "My mother let him in. Don't worry, I kicked him right back out."

"After he read my book." Granny's eyes narrowed. "And he said he liked it?"

"He did." I hid a smile. "Although he didn't get to read all of it. I could send it over to him, I guess."

14

"Don't bother." Granny glanced around. "Are we here? Where's this package we need to pick up?"

I pulled into the parking lot of the public library and parked in the northwest corner as Natalya had instructed. Granny didn't know, but inside the package were comic books, new underwear and socks, and several DVDs of Marvel movies. We were delivering it anonymously to a group home about ten miles from here. If Granny thought we were part of a rogue offshoot of the CIA, even better.

I got out and helped Granny get her walker before we slowly approached the art wall on the north side of the library. Symmetrical lines made up cement squares of all sizes in a pattern that jutted out like a 3D image. Natalya had tucked our cardboard box in one of the squares.

"Hold on," Granny barked out as I went to reach for it. She pulled an old Kodak camera out of her big leather purse and began taking pictures of a confused mother walking with her kids nearby, their arms laden with books.

 "That's right, lady. Keep on walkin'." Granny moved a shuffle closer to them and took more pictures. "There's no sneaking up on this woman."

"Sorry," I mouthed really big, earning me an irritated and bewildered look from the mom. Thankfully, Granny looked like the least threatening spy ever, and they moved along.

After that, everything went according to plan. Natalya followed behind us, I used some evasive maneuvers to "ditch" our tail, and the package was successfully delivered to the group home's doorstep. Crisis averted. We'd saved the world again.

"I could use a ladies room to freshen up," Granny declared. She was too much of a lady to ever admit to actually needing a bathroom for its true purpose. So, I drove us back toward my house to kill the last hour before Granny needed to be back for her meds and bedtime. That way, I could cook us dinner, rather than stopping off for the fast food garbage Granny preferred.

"Is that your good-for-nothing neighbor?" Granny asked, holding up her trusty Kodak when we pulled up and I turned into the carport.

Sure enough, Connor was taking his garbage can back to his side of the duplex. He stopped and stared right back at us. Click. Click. Click. I wondered how many confused faces Granny had captured with that thing. Probably a lot.

CHAPTER 4

CONNOR

Nothing was going to ruin my good mood today. One quarter of my finals were over. Everyone from my study group had shown up last night, and we'd hit the books until nobody could focus on the page and I sent them all home.

Dental school had been a long, grueling slog of exams that came in never-ending waves. I'd been memorizing and cramming so many facts into my brain for so long, I couldn't remember life before it. Not to mention the lab work and clinicals. Year four had been as brutal as everyone said it would be, but it was almost over, and I was not about to fail my final exams.

I did well today, and I'd do well tomorrow, and by this weekend, all I'd have to worry about was picking which dental practice to join up with so I could start paying off my student loans.

That was why I smiled at the wrinkled prune who stared me down while snapping pictures of me from the passenger seat of Melissa's car.

Would Melissa get out and approach me? The two times I'd seen her since her birthday party had been brief and one-sided. Basically, I waved, and she pretended not to see me.

It would be a little bit harder to keep up her avoidance right now, considering the company she was keeping.

"Young man, you get over here," the lady called out.

Oh yeah, there was no avoiding me now. Melissa knew it. She was chewing on that gorgeous bottom lip of hers like it tasted good. I bet it did. I loved her wild curls, and her curves, and her innocent brown eyes that had filled with fire when she spotted me reading in her arm chair. I had a hunch it was her favorite spot in her whole house.

Yeah, Melissa was off-limits, but Natalya wasn't here, my roommate, Rob, wasn't here, and didn't I deserve a little bonus for all my hard work today? Besides, I'd been summoned.

"Hi. Um, would you like some help?" I went to take the walker out of Melissa's hands once I realized what she was doing and why her companion hadn't gotten out of the car yet even though Melissa had opened up the passenger-side door for her.

Melissa pulled the walker closer. "I got it. I know how it unlocks."

"Okay." I held my hands up in surrender. "So, is this Granny?"

"Wouldn't you like to know." The woman slowly stood, holding onto the car frame for support, and then she pointed a long, bony finger at me. "Are you the young man who didn't help Melissa move in? She saw you watching through the window. What are all those muscles for if you can't lift anything with them?"

"Granny," Melissa murmured, turning red.

She wasn't any redder than I was. I ducked my head. "I'm sorry. I had to study that day."

"Hmph." Granny waved me aside and slowly made her way towards the door off the carport, using the walker. "Are you going to do anything about this yard, or were you too busy studying to notice how terrible it is?"

My good day was losing its goodness fast. In less than a minute, this woman had managed to poke holes in places I

18

couldn't defend like she was a high-powered prosecutor taking down a defense witness.

"The yard was like this when I bought it." It sounded weak to my own ears, but it was all I had. Putting in a yard was expensive and time-consuming. So, I just hadn't done it.

"And when was that?"

"Last year. Well, it was nice to meet you. I'll see you two later."

"Going so soon?" Granny cackled. "That's good because Melissa here isn't single, and I know that's the only reason you came over with that hopeful look in your eye. She's engaged to my grandson. He's a hero, you know. He witnessed a robbery and had to go into hiding."

"Into the witness protection program?" I asked, goosebumps raising up all over my arms.

Melissa's chin raised a little at my mocking tone. "Yes."

Oh, this was bad. I'd read the situation all wrong. The fiancé wasn't a lie Natalya made up, but Melissa's own ghosting story. I was suddenly seeing Melissa in a whole new light, one not nearly as flattering. Warning signs were going up everywhere. Melissa had been ghosted by a desperate, desperate man. He'd wanted away from her badly enough to ditch his own grandmother.

I knew first-hand what that kind of desperation felt like. I had never known someone so wholly tone-deaf to the word 'no' as Natalya. At first, needing space had been a matter of not failing out of year two of dental school. But then, I'd needed space because the more I pulled away, the harder she held on. She was jealous of every woman who talked to me. We had the 'I'm-breaking-up-with-you' talk four times, and it never stuck. I finally told her I was moving and never coming back. I blocked her number and swapped apartments with a friend for the semester. I stopped going to the same place for coffee. I changed my pharmacy and grocery store.

Three weeks later, she pulled up behind me in the drive-thru at Taco Bell. I'd been betrayed by my need for tacos and the person ahead of me who couldn't decide what to order.

Natalya had left her car and stalked over to mine. "Visiting Arizona again, Connor?"

I was too tired to lie. Too tired and too hungry. "I just want a hard taco supreme, Nat. Okay, actually, I want four of them. And I want extra mild sauce to take home. It's good on burritos."

She'd blinked at me and then her face turned tomato red and angry. "I never want to see you again, Connor Harwood."

"Fine by me."

Those were our last words to each other. Until Melissa's birthday party—the one thrown by Melissa's mom. Another red flag I'd almost ignored.

Maybe being a bad neighbor was exactly what this situation called for. Being un-neighborly had saved me from another clingy relationship. What a relief.

"You called it, Granny. I'm no catch. I don't volunteer to move stuff if I can help it, and I don't care about my yard. There's no H.O.A. here, so it makes no difference to me." I gave them a salute and jogged back to my house.

The sad thing was, I'd totally been planning to put in a yard as a graduation present to myself. I'd even talked my brother and sister into coming to help once they were on summer break. Now it would look like I did it all out of guilt. Whatever. That would be even better. Another reason for Melissa Cooke and her granny to look down on me. I'd make sure they had lots of reasons.

CHAPTER 5

MELISSA

I stepped out of the shower on Saturday night and dried off on autopilot. I'd been in a funk for days. My mind kept going over and over Granny chewing out Connor and the way he'd looked at me when Granny told him about Damien.

There were two types of people in this world, I'd decided. And I could sort them out based on the way they reacted to my fiancé's story.

Trusting, good-hearted people immediately sympathized with my plight. People like my parents, who I could tell were quietly concerned, but supportive. People like Natalya. She'd cried with me, taken on helping with Granny, and had even taught Buster and Sarge to not pee on everything and to sit and stay.

And then there were people like Connor. He had seen the truth right away, because he was cynical, and pessimistic, and understood what was wrong with men. It was because of his criminal nature, I was sure. People who did suspicious things were naturally suspicious of others.

There had to be a sinister reason for all the cars coming and going from Connor's house. Scalping tickets? Cooking drugs? Selling organs? My mind was going wild with possible answers. Then there was the fact that I'd never seen Connor's roommate. As far as I could tell, the guy came and went at odd hours. They were both probably doing weird illegal things. Good. I'd make them move far, far away after I found out what they were up to.

I yawned. Tomorrow, I'd do some investigating. The real kind, not the fake investigating I did with Granny. Buster was waiting for me when I climbed into bed in my most comfortable pajamas. I turned off the lamp and rolled over, hugging him closer as I tried to fall asleep. It wasn't sad to go to bed at nine o'clock on a Saturday night. It was sensible. Connor was the sad one, even though I could hear what sounded like a party going on next door. It was probably a drug dealer party.

But were the other drug dealers as good-looking as Connor? No way. Not possible. That was the last thought I remembered having before shooting up out of bed with a start.

Buster was awake too. He cocked his ears and gave a little whine. Was that? Yes, it was the sound of bongo drums coming through the wall. Bongo drums! How did I know? We did a six-week unit on them in music class in the sixth grade. We watched videos of people playing the bongo drums. We made home-made bongo drums out of oatmeal containers. If you were really, really good in class, you could get a turn on the real things. Then my brother wanted a set, and because it was Christmastime and my parents were out of their minds, they bought him one. Even at age twelve, it had been bongo overkill, and ever since then, when I got really stressed, the bongos would play in my head.

But this was no anxiety-induced illusion. It was right next door. I threw off the covers and slid into my slippers, not really sure what I planned to do, but knowing I couldn't listen to that racket all night. Maybe Connor was doing it on purpose. Maybe he had mined my background to find the exact thing that would torture me because Granny had been mean to him. Newsflash: Granny was mean to everyone. Well, everyone except me.

Buster followed me out the door, giving me a don't-leave-me-whine, so I picked up the little guy and warned him to let me do all the talking. Sarge was still passed out on the floor. As guard dogs, these two failed.

I channeled all my bad thoughts about Connor into determination as I marched over there, starting with the memory of him watching us empty the U-Haul and not daring to step outside. He had probably been afraid someone might get ideas about him being friendly, or decent, or assume his nicely-built body could have real-world use. Jerk. Gym rat. Hot loser.

I knocked firmly and waited. The drums continued, but I heard someone shushing someone else, and then the door opened.

It was Connor who answered, of course. He leaned on the door frame, casually taking me in, and then cocked his head. "Can I help you?" No remorse. No regret. He was happy I was annoyed. Happy, happy, happy.

Ba-dum, ba-dum, ba-dum, dum, dum went the drums behind him. Between my rising anger and the ceaseless rhythm, my brain conveniently dropped everything I'd planned to say. I stared past Connor at the blond guy sitting behind the bongos in a wife-beater tank top. His face was the picture of bliss, like he could drum forever in his own personal heaven. He had a microphone trained on the drums. That's why the sound had pulsed through the wall like they were right next to me. A few people sat around him on folding chairs, bobbing their heads along. I needed to pack up and move immediately before this weird vibe infected my side of the structure. No, *they* needed to move I reminded myself, and take their drums and stupidity with them.

"Is that your roommate?" I asked.

"Yeah, that's Rob. Look, if you wanted to come in, all you had to do was ask."

That's what he thought I wanted? I stood up straighter and leaned into Connor's face. "You think that's why I'm here? That I'm angling for an invitation from you? The turn-down-your-music lady, with no makeup and my slippers on, holding a dog, is dying to get in? Ooh, can I get an invite to your super lame party? Bongo drum solos that never end are my favorite!"

Somewhere in my speech, the drums had stopped, but my volume had remained the same. Loud. I didn't realize it until it got eerily quiet, and then several people booed me.

"She's gonna call the cops," someone whispered amid all the glares.

Connor ran a hand through his wavy dark hair before giving everyone a calm-it-down wave and stepping out onto the porch with me. He shut the door firmly behind us.

"Look, I get it. You're forever *not* single. Natalya and your granny cleared that up for me. I'm sorry I invited you in. I am not coming on to you, and I won't in the future. You can count on it."

Forever *not* single. That again? It was all too much, and at that moment, my tear ducts decided I hadn't been humiliated quite enough. I hid my face in Buster's fur so Connor wouldn't see me pulling it together, but when I looked up I could tell I wasn't fooling him.

"Hey, are you okay?" he asked, reaching out as if to touch my shoulder and then drawing his hand back when Buster gave him a warning yip.

"You're the worst neighbor ever," I said, but with no heat this time. My anger had lost a fight with my embarrassment. I'd never been booed before. If anyone deserved to do some booing, it was me.

"Are you sure *I'm* the worst?" Connor pulled out his phone and checked it. "It's ten-thirty on a Saturday night. I promise we would've been done and my house silent by midnight."

"It's good to know you have standards." Ah, anger might have left me, but I still had sarcasm.

"Um, you also crashed my roommate's debut concert to kick off his album release. I know bongo drums aren't your favorite." He bit back a laugh. "But some people like them.

Some people even try to be supportive of their friend's endeavors."

"Oh."

CHAPTER 6

CONNOR

Be strong, man. Melissa's beautiful dark curls and elephant print pajama pants were luring me into her siren song. What was wrong with me, if the best way to get my attention was to storm into a party wearing slippers and insulting everyone?

I had almost convinced myself I was indifferent to her, and now here she was again. It didn't help that Rob was back to banging on the bongos, and I had zero interest in returning for the end of his concert.

She said something I didn't quite catch, so I leaned closer. Just for hearing purposes, of course. "What was that?"

Melissa narrowed her eyes at me, like she could read the lies I was telling myself. "Why haven't I seen your roommate before tonight?"

"Were you hoping to?"

"No. It just seems suspicious that I've never seen him."

"He's a weird dude who keeps weird hours."

"Is he the reason all the strange cars are coming and going from your place all the time?" She looked irritated, but there was expectation threaded through her question, too. Like she hoped it was my roommate who was the shady one and not me. Why?

And then it hit me. She was attracted to me, just like I was attracted to her. Miss Forever *Not* Single secretly liked me. No, no, no. That wouldn't work.

I ducked my head, channeling every after school special I'd ever watched growing up, even shuffling back and forth like the question made me nervous. "Nah, that's me. It's just to make a few more bucks, and then I swear I won't do it anymore."

Melissa backed up from me, as I knew she would. "Okay then, goodnight."

"You won't say anything to anyone, will you?"

Her eyes widened before she attempted a look of casual indifference. "As long as it stops."

"It will. I just have to get rid of this last stash." Maybe adding that last part was a bit too much. I didn't want to get falsely arrested. I just wanted her to turn around and never talk to me again. She was too tempting—as all hot messes were.

Melissa was almost to her front door when a vehicle honked from the street, making us both jump. "Yoo-hoo! Are you Connor Harwood? I'm here to pick up the set of back scratchers you had for sale in the Facebook yard sale group."

An older couple in a minivan had stopped in front of our duplex. They couldn't park because of the cars in front, so they were idling in the road with the passenger-side window down. The woman looked at us expectantly.

"Nope, wrong house," I called back. It about killed me to send them off. Who else was going to buy a bag of used wooden backscratchers for fifteen bucks?

"No, you have the right place," Melissa called out. She turned to stare me down. "Go get their backscratchers, loser."

"I'm still a drug dealer," I said.

"Sure you are. I should have known when I heard the bongos from your super lame party."

"They're buying drugs from me."

"The minivan people? And they know your real name?"

"Connor Harwood is my dealer name."

Melissa laughed, and I loved the sound a little too much. "Look, I don't know why you're so determined to prove you're a terrible person, but whatever. I'm going to bed."

"I am a terrible person." I was. I was falling into her trap right now. I wanted to follow her home. Even if it meant faking my death later to get away from her.

Instead, I went inside to find the stupid backscratchers.

CHAPTER 7

MELISSA

Natalya came over on Sunday night to help me plan Granny's next few adventures. Sometimes our brainstorming sessions just meant we watched several episodes of Investigation Miami, which was a truly dumb show that redeemed itself only by its entertaining plots and overabundance of eye candy. I could watch the super-hot Officer Florez shine his flashlight around old, abandoned buildings all day.

When Natalya asked about my week, I purposely didn't mention the little concert at Connor's place. Natalya didn't need more ammunition for her utter hatred of the guy, and I had a hunch his weird behavior toward me had more to do with my best friend than it did with me.

Natalya was the most loveable person I'd ever known. Loyal, steady, and go-with-the-flow. Except when it came to men. Her dating track record in the two years I'd known her was not stellar. Despite being the most beautiful and sweet woman a guy could ask for, things always ended badly. Mementos were burned in effigy, the guys names were never to be mentioned again, and there was crying. Lots of crying.

But because she was my best friend, and Connor had already proved what a jerk he was, I had to err on the side of believing her when she said he'd done her wrong.

"Okay, I'm thinking like a super spy. What if I left a keycard in a safety deposit box for you and Granny to find?" Natalya suggested.

"We did that already, remember? Except it was an invisible ink pen and notepad. That was fun."

"Right." Natalya tapped her chin with her pen. "Okay, this might be a little out there, but what if someone's chickens suddenly went missing?"

"I can't do the Bigfoot thing again, Nat. Granny's walker doesn't do well in the woods."

She laughed. "Okay, what if—?" She cut off abruptly, and her eyes went to a spot behind me on the wall. And then she began screaming. A lot.

I scrambled to my feet and turned to see a wolf spider on steroids hanging out next to my light switch. It was so big it had to be part tarantula. Maybe a tarantula and a wolf spider had a forbidden love affair and this was the result.

"Kill it now!" Natalya shrieked.

Sarge lifted his head and howled in protest at all the noise. Buster turned in circles and then peed on the linoleum. He still had trouble sometimes when he got overexcited.

"Nat, stop. You're scaring the dogs."

Natalya picked up her heavy wedge sandal before I could stop her and chucked it at the wall. The spider moved two inches, causing Natalya to take up screaming again. Now I had a small dent, a very skittish spider, a wet spot to clean up, and two freaked out dogs barking.

"You have to stop screaming," I demanded. "You'll bring Connor over here."

That stopped her. Natalya let out a shuddering breath. "He won't come because he's a coward and a deserter." But she still glanced at the door, looking worried.

"I'll get the spider. You stay over there." I grabbed a plastic cup off the counter and took slow and easy steps over to the wall. I didn't want the thing making a break for the ceiling.

"Why do you have a cup?" Natalya asked slowly, as if I were juggling hand grenades and needed to be talked out of it.

"Because I'm taking him outside."

"Him?"

"Wolf spiders don't bite. Usually. And they're not venomous. He can go live out in my yard and eat crickets."

"What if it's a recluse? Those can kill you."

"He's too hairy to be a recluse spider."

"Do you even hear yourself?"

I did. And it wasn't like I was always a defender of pests. I just didn't like squishing things. And I appreciated a creature who was calm under pressure. Wolf spiders retreated when confronted. I could respect that.

I scraped the cup against the wall until Mr. Spider dropped into it, and then I headed for the door. I was so intent on watching the spider in the cup that I didn't notice Connor standing on my porch when I opened the door. It startled me just enough to make the cup in my hands jump, enough to launch a spider right onto his chest.

CHAPTER 8

CONNOR

"Glahh!" That was the high-pitched noise that left my throat when I realized I had a gigantic, hairy spider clinging to my shirt. "You're a monster!"

I backtracked into the yard, holding the fabric of my shirt away from my skin, and all the while Melissa followed me with the incriminating cup in her hands.

It was payback of the most diabolical kind, her screaming to draw me over there, just so she could throw a spider at me.

Every time I thought I had the woman figured out, she changed the rules. I didn't know if anything else was in that cup, but I didn't want to find out.

"Wait!" She edged closer, making me back up faster, and the farther we moved from the porchlights the less I could see. My ankle twisted as I hit an old gopher hole, and I went down, scraping my palms in the dirt.

I quickly scrambled to my feet and held my arms out at my sides in a frozen position, afraid if I moved, the spider would move up my neck and bite me. It was no longer on my chest where I'd last seen it, but that was far from comforting. It could be anywhere. It could be on my pants. *Oh, please don't let it be on my pants.* I shivered and squeezed my eyes shut. "This is war, Melissa. Just wait and see what creepy-crawly thing ends up on you after this."

"It was an accident. Calm down and let me search you. I'm trying to help." She put down the cup and pulled out her phone, turning on flashlight mode.

I held still as she shined the flashlight up and down my body. She stepped closer and ran her hand down the folds of my shirt, making me shiver. She smelled like citrus blossoms and spun sugar. It was all part of her evil plan to break me down step by step, I told myself.

Then she lifted my shirt up and flashed her phone on my skin. After checking there, her eyes glanced up, meeting mine before she quickly looked away. Was she blushing?

"How was throwing a spider on me an accident?" I asked in a voice I hoped was calm.

Melissa moved to my back and checked there. "I was taking it outside. I didn't know you were standing there. You startled me." There was a little wobble to her voice that set my heart beating faster than it already was.

Was our close proximity affecting her as much as it was affecting me? My brain followed the movement of her hands, first on my shoulder blades, and then where she touched my arms to lower them. She ran her warm fingers across my forearms before pulling away, which was completely unnecessary and yet totally welcome. I'd officially lost my mind. She could dump a bunch of new spiders on me and I'd thank her and report for inspection.

"I think it's gone. I'm sorry. I meant to just throw him out in the yard."

"So he could find his way into my place next?" I raised an eyebrow at her.

"That was the hope." She grinned. "I can't believe you're afraid of spiders."

"I'm afraid of spider hitchhikers. There's a difference."

"Hey!" a familiar voice called from the porch. Natalya stood under the porchlight holding Melissa's little dog. "Tell Connor to go away now. It's not like he came in time to save us from anything anyway."

"I stopped to put pants on." I'd been about to go to bed. In hindsight, throwing on a pair of track pants and a T-shirt had saved me from skin-on-skin contact with an arachnid. That was a win in my book.

"Good to know you care more about your pants than our safety," Natalya huffed. "We could have been dying in here."

"I'm glad you put on pants," Melissa murmured next to me. "For what it's worth."

She began to laugh and so did I, making Natalya even more irritated with us. I waited until they were both inside before going home, where I stripped down and showered before I felt confident enough to go to bed, knowing I was spider-free.

CHAPTER 9

←——————————→

MELISSA

It turned out I didn't need to plan an adventure for Monday evening, because as soon as I mentioned my intentions to buy and plant grass seed this week, Granny was all about going with me to shop.

I should have known not to say anything to her about it. The only thing Granny liked more than solving crimes was a shopping trip where someone else was spending the money, and she had free rein to give advice.

She read her latest letter from Damien on the way to the home improvement store. This week, his postmark was from Mississippi. Maybe he truly was wandering the country like a nomad, looking for more unsuspecting women to con. Maybe his sweet letters of fake devotion were just practice. I didn't read the ones he sent me anymore. It was better not to let him in my head.

I got Granny in a motorized scooter at the front of the store, and we headed over to the lawn and garden section.

"If you don't keep it continually watered, the grass will die as soon as it comes up," Granny warned. "You really should have planted Bermuda grass last month when the temperatures were down in the eighties. It's probably too hot now."

"Yeah, I know." She'd read the planting instructions off the same display sign as I had, but it didn't hurt to hear it twice. Granny had so few people to lecture these days; it might as well be me.

Granny cruised ahead in her motorized shopping cart to the hoses. "You should have measured your yard so you know what length to buy."

"I'll go long to be safe." I threw a 100 foot hose in my cart and continued down the aisle to the sprinkler section. A professionally installed sprinkler system would have been nice, but then, so would a backyard pool with a rock waterfall and a swim-up bar. Neither of those things would be happening on a receptionist's salary, but a girl could dream.

I grabbed a couple of twenty-dollar metal oscillating sprinklers off the shelf and dropped them in the cart on top of the hose.

"We should have gotten the grass seed first, Melissa. The biggest and heaviest items should go on the bottom of the cart."

"I'll rearrange. It will be my workout for today."

"Well, all right." Granny scootered ahead to the outdoor section where the grass seed was, and I hurried to follow with my cart. Knowing the grass seed bags needed to go in first didn't stop me from being distracted by all the flowers and succulents on display. I'd have to come back for them. I wanted some taller shrubbery to flank my front door.

I reluctantly continued on, but my attention caught on the back of a guy's head as he strolled down the next aisle. His cart had a couple of plants in it. Was it Connor? He turned to look at something, showing me his gorgeous profile. Shoot. It totally was him. I needed to find Granny before she spotted my neighbor and gave him the third degree about the yard again. The last thing I wanted was another altercation, this time in public. She'd probably try to make him pay for my purchases and become my indentured servant boy. Not that those were bad things…. But no.

Staying low, I darted off towards the grass seed display. Granny had abandoned her motorized scooter and stood poking at the bags, making harrumphing noises at the ones that were leaking seed. I was pretty sure she was the reason they were leaking.

"Sloppy packaging," she muttered.

I loaded a fifty-pound bag of grass seed in the cart, right on top of the sprinklers, at the moment not caring about order, or weight, or anything else.

"That bag has a hole. You need this one." Granny pointed at a seed bag, the third one down in the stack.

"This will have to work for now. My back can only take so much lifting." I glanced behind me, tracking Connor's progress. He was headed our way, but in no hurry, and thankfully, he wasn't looking in our direction.

Granny, for once, gave up her side of the argument and got in her scooter to follow me towards the registers. I took off at a jog and slid my cart in line ahead of a guy juggling tomato plants, earning me a glare. Whatever. It would all be worth it if we could just get out before Granny spotted Connor.

The attendant scanned the hose and grass seed, and with a quick swipe of my card, we were done. I hurried off with Granny at my side. Mission accomplished.

"Ma'am. Wait, ma'am. Ma'am, hold up." It didn't register that the store clerk was hollering at me until the steady whoosh of grass seed and the quickly approaching footsteps put it all together for me, along with one pesky detail I'd missed in my hurry. She hadn't scanned the sprinklers buried under the seed bag because I hadn't told her about them. And they'd just pierced the underside of my grass bag, which was now leaving a trail along the parking lot.

"The bag is leaking," Granny so helpfully pointed out. "It's leaking a lot."

The clerk who had followed us stared at the grass seed all over the ground and then at my cart, clearly not sure what to do now that she had my attention. She'd been running on pure instinct, as had I. "Uh, ma'am, are there items under the bag of grass seed? If so, you'll need to pay for them."

"Yes. I'll come back and pay for the sprinklers," I said. "I forgot about those."

The clerk nodded. "Sorry about your grass seed."

No offer to swap it out, I noted. That was sixty dollars only the birds would get to enjoy. And all so I wouldn't run into my stupid neighbor.

I turned my cart around and stopped to flip the bag over, careful not to put it down on top of the sprinkler heads this time. It wouldn't save all of it, but better to keep what I could.

"I have some duct tape," the clerk offered with a shrug.

I followed her back to the counter where several other customers watched me run my card again and tape up my grass seed bag. Out of the corner of my eye, I saw a familiar profile duck around, grab something from behind the counter, and dart out again.

"Was that—?" Granny began to ask.

"Don't say it. I don't want to know."

"Okay. I won't say it was your handsome but useless neighbor."

"Thanks, Granny."

"Are you going to make him plant this grass seed for you?"

"Nope. My mom is coming over tomorrow to help. We'll be fine."

Granny sighed, clearly disappointed in my lack of enthusiasm for confrontation.

We left with everything paid for this time, but outside I stopped short at the sight of Connor bent over my grass seed trails with a little dustpan and broom he'd swiped from behind the sales counter. He was sweeping it all up into a plastic shopping bag.

"He's stealing your seed," Granny hissed. "He wants it for himself, the cheapo."

I didn't agree, but I also didn't want to stay there watching and speculating with the most suspicious woman I knew. So I pushed onward to my car, loaded up my purchases, and drove off with my nerves feeling like they'd been tossed in a blender.

When I got home after dropping Granny off, there were two shopping bags full of recovered grass seed on my porch, another large bag in a brand-new package, a seed spreader I'd forgotten to buy, and two bags of mulch.

Why had he done all that? Connor was supposed to be my terrible neighbor, and I was supposed to hate him. Or at least find him annoying and despicable. But I wasn't feeling any of those things at the moment, and I didn't know what to do about it. I'd have to thank him later, when I wasn't tempted to give him a big hug. Hugging him would be super gross. Because…. reasons. I'd come up with some. I would not think about his strong arms or my fingers running over them, pretending to look for a spider I knew had scampered off. Nope. I wasn't thinking about any of that.

CHAPTER 10

CONNOR

I peered through the blinds again, craning my neck to confirm that Melissa hadn't left for work. Yep, her car was still there. As tired as I was of waiting in here, knowing the morning would only get hotter, I didn't dare step outside and start on the yard yet.

It was better if Melissa came home from work this afternoon and thought some yard fairy had descended. I'd have plausible deniability. Both of us could pretend I didn't enjoy swooping in to help her like I had last night. Denial had been working pretty well for me so far. For example, right now I wasn't thinking about what her reaction might be to seeing a seeded yard, or the gravel all cleaned up, or the flower beds planted. I wasn't considering how happy it would make her.

Nope. I was doing this all for me. Because I was a selfish and terrible person who wanted a nice yard just for me.

My roommate, Rob, stumbled into the front room and peered at me through his squinty eyes. "What day is it?"

"Tuesday."

"Are you sure? You're never here on Tuesdays."

"I am today." I turned back to the window, listening to Rob rummage around in the kitchen. As little time as we spent together, I knew his routine. He'd shove handfuls of cereal in his mouth straight from the box, take a long drink of water from any cup on the counter, and then stumble back to bed until noon. He did have a job at a used bookstore, but it was more of a hobby for him, kind of like his new bongo album. His real money came from a lawsuit he'd won against one of those medical testing facilities. Whether or not they did anything to him worth suing over was a question I asked myself a lot. Sometimes I thought nobody could be that weird without medical intervention.

Hurry, Melissa. What was going on? She always left by seven-thirty. My brother and sister would be coming to help me any minute, and if they didn't have something to do, they'd be bickering in here with me. I was edgy enough as it was.

This no-school and no-work thing was so foreign to me. Even before dental school, I'd always worked. My dad owned a heavy equipment rental business, and from the time I could hold a wrench I'd been tinkering on machines with him. Now for the first time ever, I had nothing to study for and nowhere to go. Sure, I had interviews lined up, but those were for next week.

Today, I was as free as a kid on his first day of summer. Well, except that I was stuck waiting on Melissa to leave for work.

A sedan pulled up to the curb, and I watched a woman get out and adjust the purple visor on her head and straighten her oversized T-shirt. Even with the big sunglasses covering half her face, I knew who it was. Melissa's mother was dressed like someone ready to do some yard work. Not good. This was not good for my morning plans at all.

She walked purposefully up to Melissa's door and out of my view, leaving me with a decision to make. That decision deadline got more urgent after Melissa and her mom stepped out into the yard together trailed by Melissa's two dogs. The two women began raking gravel out of the way. Over time, the gravel had meandered into the dead grass sections until everything everywhere was dead and patchy rock. Facing the hideousness of it all would've been a lot easier without their judging eyes. My plan to become a yard fairy had just disintegrated.

Pacing in front of the window made my indecision worse, but I couldn't stop myself. I had plants that needed to come out of their plastic pots and get water and sun. I hadn't bought Melissa extra seed and a spreader so I could watch her work all day, but I also hadn't planned to go out of my way to spend time with her or her mother. I had walls that needed to remain intact. Neighborly walls that didn't allow for friendship, or courtship, or making out with her on her couch. *Okay, reel it in, thoughts.*

My siblings pulled up to the curb in Parker's truck, and my destiny was cemented. They had Parker's best friend, Clay, with them. At least I'd have plenty of help.

I jogged outside and met up with my brother before he could ask what Melissa and her mom were doing in the yard. Parker wasn't known for his subtlety. The kid was scrappy. The shortest of the Harwood siblings, with the most to prove to the world, at least in his own mind.

"Your neighbors are helping us?" Parker asked, nodding at them. "Are they new? I thought nobody lived on the other side of the duplex."

I turned to look at Melissa and gave her an awkward smile to match the one she had aimed at me. She couldn't hear us, but she obviously could tell we were talking about her.

"Yeah, they're new. We're all going to work together."

"Cool." My sister, Lauren, breezed passed me and knelt down to say hello to the dogs. They wagged their tails and ate up the attention. Soon, Lauren was clearing out rock with Melissa and talking up a storm. Probably telling stories about me. My only solace was that Lauren didn't have much dirt. She was twelve years younger than me. All my annoying stages were too far back for her to remember.

I assigned Parker to rip out the dead cottonwood tree and gave Clay the task of prepping the flower beds. I went and got my own rake and hoe from the small shed in the back and hurried around the side of the house, almost running into Melissa. She had a small smudge of dirt on her cheek and I resisted the urge to wipe it away for her. Not that I could have with my hands full of tools.

"Did you ditch work for this?" I asked. Telling her I would have done it all myself was on the tip of my tongue, but I held it back.

"I took a personal day. I had a bunch stored up."

"It was nice of your mom to come help."

"Yeah. My dad had to work today, but he said he'd come by tomorrow and do anything we didn't get done."

"Great." I'd make sure there was nothing left.

"What about you? No studying today?" she asked.

"Nope. I'm officially graduated from dental school."

"Dental school? That's awesome. And now I'm realizing how little I know about you." She smiled, and her eyes sparkled like they held a secret. "Well, I do know a few things, thanks to your sister. Is it true you asked Felicia Rae Gomez to Prom in a YouTube video?"

"That was... a bet. Actually, 'dare' is a better word." I was going to kill Lauren.

"I think it's sweet. I loved her in *Haunted High School* back in the day. I even had a HSH bumper sticker on my car."

My face, already hot from the sun, burned even more. "It wasn't the *Haunted High School* thing for me. She was the voice of Tez Dreamstore in *Aliens and Convenience Stores*." My explanation was making me sound even more like a nerd, but I couldn't seem to stop. "Not that you'd know what that is."

"It was a video game, right?"

"Yeah."

Melissa nodded. "So, um, did she ever respond?"

"I got a letter." Probably one written by her team, but it had been nice all the same. I knew exactly where it was in my box of memorabilia, but it wasn't about to see the light of day anytime soon. "And no, I didn't take Felicia Rae Gomez to Prom. Should I check with your mom and see if she has any fun stories about you?"

Melissa lifted her chin. "Go right ahead, tough guy."

I stepped closer. "You sound a little nervous. Why is that?"

"No reason."

"No fun stories about you she could share?"

"Not any good ones."

Lies. All lies. Her face was telling me there were a lot of juicy stories her mom would be happy to share. What had Melissa been like back in high school?

I got lost in her big brown eyes for a moment. Realizing our little staring contest was getting a bit too charged for me, I ducked around her with my tools and got to work. I was letting down my guard again. She was all wrong for me, and I wouldn't let my instincts be fooled into thinking otherwise.

CHAPTER 11

MELISSA

I tugged at the dead tree in the middle of the yard, but it wouldn't budge. We'd have to dig deeper. Stinking dead roots.

I stepped back and let Parker shovel out more dirt. "Connor has never mentioned you," he huffed out between shovelfuls. "Which is weird because you're really good-looking."

I blinked at him, trying to figure out if he was teasing me. But just like when he asked if my mom and I were sisters, it was impulse coming out of his mouth, and not flattery. Good thing his impulses happened to be flattering. Sort of.

"Does Connor always mention when women are good-looking?" I asked, trying not to laugh.

"Well, yeah. All guys do." Parker and Clay exchanged fist bumps.

Lauren, raking rock nearby, gave me a look of long-suffering, but I had a feeling she purposely chose the kind of torture that allowed her to hang out with her older brother and his cute friend.

I glanced over at Connor, who had kept himself extremely busy ever since our side of the house interaction. He wouldn't work within ten feet of me, or even look at me. I had embarrassed him by mentioning his childhood crush on Felicia

Rae Gomez, and enjoyed it thoroughly, and if he knew what else his siblings had revealed about him, he might actually die of humiliation. Apparently, he'd been quite the geek in high school, despite his strong build and his success on the football field. I lapped up every story they had to tell.

But maybe it wasn't embarrassment keeping Connor away from me. Maybe it was the way our interactions always turned a bit flirty. With Natalya as my best friend, he probably preferred to keep his distance from us both.

Parker and I tried tugging the tree out, and this time it gave way with a mighty snap of dead tree roots and a spray of dirt. Unfortunately, summer wasn't a good time to plant trees. We'd have to wait until fall to replace the thing. But I could be content with grass and flowers for now.

Working as a team, we accomplished more than I'd ever imagined. By the time we broke for lunch, the lawn was seeded and watered, the flower bed was all planted, and the gravel had been tamed into its own section behind the cement curbing.

Parker gathered up the plant containers and seed bags and took them to the trash can by the curb. "We're gonna bail, Connor. Glad you're not the eyesore of the neighborhood anymore."

"Yes, it all looks nice," my mom said, smoothing over Parker's dig. "I'm going home, too. Well, unless you still need me." She glanced between me and Connor and smiled. "But I'm sure you two can take it from here."

"Thanks, Mom." I pleaded with my eyes for her to not insinuate anything further, which only made her smile bigger. "He's a cute one," she whispered when I hugged her goodbye.

"Not happening," I whispered back.

My words couldn't have been truer. Connor escaped inside his door the second she pulled away from the curb. No wave, no parting words between us. Nothing.

I called for Sarge and Buster, who were happily sniffing the new yard and trying to drink from the sprinklers without getting sprayed in the face. They needed their water bowls and some air conditioning.

"Come on, guys." I stalked into my side of the duplex and took care of them before heading into the shower, feeling broody. Connor's avoidance today bothered me. Yeah, he was embarrassed about the yard. And he didn't want to spend time with the best friend of his ex-girlfriend. Both of those things were understandable, and yet I was still ticked off.

I had the rest of my day off ahead of me, and Connor knew it. He'd bailed faster than a man in a sinking boat, afraid I'd try to take more of his time and space without anyone else there as a buffer. The thought of spending time with me was abhorrent to him.

I should invite Natalya over just to make things that much more awkward. And have a picnic on his doorstep.

Instead, I dressed, teased my curls, put on a cute sundress, and dodged the sprinklers that were hitting the porch as I walked over to his door. I had no plan. I was just fueled by a lot of dumb stubbornness and free time.

Connor's blond roommate answered after two knocks, wearing sweats and a Beatles T-shirt. "Oh, it's you," he said, rolling his eyes. "I'm not going to stop practicing so you can just..." He made a shooing motion with his hand. "Go back to your place."

"Stop practicing what?"

"The drums?" He moved aside so I could see his bongos in the corner of their living room. Right. Without the microphone trained on them, the noise didn't carry through the wall. While we were working on the yard all morning, he must have been in here banging on those. How nice of him.

"I'm not here about the bongos."

"Oh." He seemed to take in my appearance for the first time. "You're actually quite attractive. I don't know what Connor was talking about."

"What now?"

He scratched the back of his head and looked behind him, like he was hoping for backup that wasn't there. "I just thought... you know what? Never mind. Would you like to come in? Are you hungry? I was about to make a smoothie."

"Where's Connor?" He'd told his roommate I wasn't attractive? Maybe I did need to invest in a spider farm. Jerk. Worst neighbor ever. Girl-avoiding loser.

"He's in the shower. I'll let him know you stopped by."

A door clicked open down the hall, and seconds later, Connor walked into the front room, towel drying his dark hair and whistling. He had on a fresh T-shirt and basketball shorts.

The second he saw me at the door, the whistling stopped and he froze. "Melissa."

"Connor." My voice was not friendly, and he eyed me cautiously as he slid his feet into a pair of Nike slides. Tossing the towel he'd been holding on the arm of his couch, he came to the door and stepped out. "Let's go to lunch. Bye, Rob."

"Where are you two—?"

Connor shut the door firmly, cutting off the rest of Rob's question.

"We're going to lunch?" I asked.

"I'd like to." Connor touched his back pocket. "One moment. Stay here, please." As if I might try to follow him back inside or something. Whatever. He returned a moment later with his wallet and keys and motioned to his truck. "Ready?"

I folded my arms and stared him down. "Where are we going?"

"Are you picky or something?"

"No. I'm confused."

"Are you confused because you're not sure if you're hungry or not?"

"I'm confused because I don't know why we're going somewhere together. You told Rob I was not attractive."

He opened his mouth to rebut, but I cut him off. "Don't."

"But, I—"

"Nope. I'm good. It's not an ego thing. It's just rude to rate your neighbor on a hotness scale. And I don't want your pity lunch after you took off the second everyone left today. I get it. We're not going to be friends."

Connor looked at the ground. "So, I'm not allowed to defend myself?" He mumbled something right after it that sounded a lot like, "Not that I should."

"Why do you do that?"

"Do what?" He looked up at me, and I could see the fear. He knew exactly what I was asking about.

"Why don't you want me to like you?"

He put his hands up in a plea. "Lunch first?"

"You must be really hungry. Hang on a second." I went into my place and grabbed my purse. There was no way I'd be letting Connor pay for me. This was not a date, just a fact-finding mission with food.

CHAPTER 12

←——————————→

CONNOR

This was not a date, and I knew Melissa felt the same way, because she'd elbowed me out of the way to pay for her sandwich and chips herself. I should have been relieved by that, but all I felt was guilt over her accusation about us not being friends. Yes, I had my reasons for keeping my prickly distance, but she didn't know that. And worse, I was starting to wonder if my reasoning had ever been valid. I needed to know things.

"Tell me about your witness protection fiancé."

"No." Melissa returned her sandwich to her tray and stared me down. "I had a question for you, and you'll answer it first before you get anything from me." The staring contest ended when she snuck a glance at her sandwich and couldn't resist picking it up for another bite. She liked her sandwich a lot more than me at the moment, even though I'd brought her to my favorite deli, which was now clearly her favorite deli. I knew she'd like the checkered table cloths and the baby farm animal décor. I just liked it for the amazing food.

"I didn't tell Rob you weren't attractive because I thought you... weren't attractive." I cleared my throat as my face heated. Now I had her attention. "I told him that because most women find him a little forward. I was trying to spare you an uncomfortable come-on from him. So, when he asked about you, I threw him off the scent, so to speak."

Melissa studied me. Several reactions crossed her face, but she didn't say anything.

"Had I known you would insult his bongo skills in front of all his friends on first meeting him, I wouldn't have bothered."

Melissa laughed. "Yeah… He's still a little ticked off about that. But he did invite me in for a smoothie right before you came to the door."

"His smoothies are the worst. You definitely dodged a bullet there."

"By going out with you instead?"

"Yeah, I guess it is sad when I'm your best option." I stole the last potato chip out of her bag, just to clinch my point.

"You don't scare me, Connor Harwood."

"I was afraid of that."

She crossed her arms and sat back. "Because of Natalya?"

"She's definitely made me cautious when it comes to women."

"Are you afraid I'm just like her, or are you afraid you'll have to hang out with her again if the two of us are friends?"

"Both?" I'd have to tread carefully here. "Tell me about your fiancé."

"No." She balled up her now-empty chip bag like it had personally offended her. "Your curiosity is not a good enough reason to open up to you, Connor. I'm not telling you just so you can be amused by it."

"I'm sorry." And I was sorry. I'd given her no reason to trust me, and the only reason I wanted to know was so I could either confirm that she'd driven a man to run, or come up with a new conclusion.

But the more I got to know Melissa, the less likely it seemed that anyone would purposely run away from her. Maybe she did have a fiancé in the witness protection program after all. Maybe she really was eternally 'not single.' The thought filled me with more dread than thinking she might be stalker material.

I was pressing my luck, but I had one more question. "Do you still love him?"

Melissa's eyes narrowed, and she leaned across the table. "Why do I get the feeling you have a hard time hearing 'no'?"

There was no point in answering that. She already had me pegged. "Ready for ice cream? There's a great place right across the park next door. We could walk."

Melissa's mouth opened to tell me no, but she paused and stared at me. "Yeah, okay. I never turn down ice cream."

"Me either."

CHAPTER 13

MELISSA

Connor and I traded off sprinkler duty, and for the rest of the week, he found an excuse to come over every evening after I got home from work. It was like he took my accusation about us not being friends as a personal challenge. The first night, he claimed he needed a break from the bongo drums. That, I could understand. We made tacos together while I introduced him to *Investigation Miami*.

The next night he claimed he couldn't watch the next episode of *Investigation Miami* without me.

By the third night, I just left my door unlocked and texted him to bring dessert. Yes, we'd exchanged numbers. But we didn't talk about being friends. We didn't touch, not even in passing while we cooked. We just co-existed while whatever battle he was fighting in his head raged on.

For some reason, he was hung up on the fiancé thing, and I couldn't decide whether it was because I wouldn't tell him what he wanted to know or because he assumed I was engaged and wanted to keep certain boundaries in place.

Natalya wanted to go to dinner and a movie on Saturday night, so I texted Connor to let him know I wouldn't be home.

He offered to feed my dogs and keep them company while I was gone. I had no idea how far that commitment went until I came in the door at eleven and he was sitting on my couch with Buster dozing on his lap. The coffee table was covered in thick stapled paper packets.

"What are you doing?"

Connor reached up and stretched, showing off his very fine triceps. Not that I was paying attention to them... much. "I'm deciding which dental practice to join up with. These are the offers."

"Oh." I sat down next to him and listened while he went through the pros and cons of each.

"It sounds like a good dilemma to have, to be honest." I was impressed that three different dental practices wanted him.

"Yeah. I guess it is." He put down the packet in his hands and turned to study me. "You smell like movie theater popcorn."

"Guilty. I almost finished off a whole bucket."

His smile at my words warmed every part of me, but it also shifted the precariously balanced friendship boat we were sitting in. I should be annoyed that he was here, but all I could think about was how much I wanted to be near him. Really near him. Not sitting and chatting, but having his hand on my knee, or his arm around my shoulder, or even an accidental brush of our hands. The butterflies gathering dust in the pit of my stomach would take just about any hint of excitement, no matter how small. But I would not make the first move. At this point, it was a matter of principle.

"I'll let you have your house back." He carefully lifted Buster off his lap and placed him on the rug at our feet. The dog let out a funny little snore, but otherwise didn't notice the change in location. "Oh, what movie did you end up seeing?" Connor asked.

"*Love is for Suckers*. It was Natalya's pick."

"How was it?"

"Meh. I would have preferred to watch dinosaurs eat people."

Connor put a hand to his chest. "A woman after my own heart."

"You are impressed by the dumbest things."

"You have no idea."

I stood and went to get the door for him. It just seemed important at the moment to let him think I wanted him to leave. While he took his time gathering his paper packets, I glanced around and noticed he'd cleaned up my kitchen. It wasn't like I'd left a sink full of dirty dishes or anything, but he'd scoured the rice pan I'd left soaking. He'd wiped down my counters. I was pretty sure he'd swept. He'd spent a lot of time here, waiting up for me. Why?

His gaze followed mine, and when our eyes returned to each other, he looked embarrassed.

"Why are you here, Connor?" I asked, not patient enough to let the mystery unfold at his pace.

"I needed a quiet place to look over these contracts. I'm sorry I stayed so late."

I continued to stare, not accepting that answer.

"What answer are you hoping for?"

"The truth." I swallowed hard. Our staring contests were always charged, now more than ever. My heart rate picked up with every second he looked at me like that—like he was torn between the obvious chemistry pulsing between us and the casual indifference he tried to convey. I saw the moment chemistry won.

He dropped the contracts back on the coffee table and stalked towards me. I braced for impact, but it didn't prepare me for his mouth taking mine, or his hands on my waist, holding me in place against the door. I dropped my hand from the door knob and gripped the back of his neck, sliding my fingers into his hair.

"I'm sorry," he murmured, moving his lips to my neck where he paused and breathed in deep. "I'm so sorry."

"What are you sorry for?"

"I do everything wrong. I'm a bad neighbor. I haven't even taken you out on a date. I've questioned everything about you, and yet all I've wanted to do since the moment I saw you was this." He kissed me again and again, and all rational thought left my brain. My limbs were like Jell-O, and I let him steady me.

"Melissa," he whispered, pulling back to look at my face. "Are you engaged? Are you in love with someone else?"

I shook my head, for once not sorry that Damien was gone for good. "He's never coming back. And if he did, I wouldn't let him."

Connor's face turned sad. "He's an idiot."

"I know." I reached up and touched Connor's lips, and he pressed a kiss into the tips of my fingers, and then the center of my palm, and then my wrist. If he was trying to capture my attention, he had it. I slipped my arms around his neck and kissed him first this time, taking the lead.

After a minute, he groaned, resting his head in the crook of my neck. "I should go. It's late and this is new. And I know we need to talk, but now is probably not the best time."

I nodded. All I wanted to do was kiss Connor until the end of forever. We'd have to wait and talk when my body wasn't flooded with a million sensations begging for more. I opened my door and pushed him out of it, making him laugh.

"Good night, Melissa."

"Good night, Connor." I shut the door and locked it before I changed my mind.

CHAPTER 14

CONNOR

My thoughts had been going in waves of excitement and panic since the moment I left Melissa's house last night.

Man, Melissa can kiss. I can't believe I almost missed out on that.

But we're neighbors, what if this doesn't work out?

What if she finds out I thought she was a potential stalker? Except, I'm more the stalker at this point. I've invited myself to her house every night this week. And I kissed her first.

I really like kissing her. I like everything about her.

What if she finds out I thought her mom was overbearing?

Okay, I still think that. But she's also a really nice lady who is good at yard work and loves her daughter. I'm a judgmental idiot.

I'm the luckiest man alive. I can't wait to see her again.

What if she changed her mind? What if she hates me?

I got out of bed and showered, knowing at some point, regardless of whether I happened to be in the panic or excitement camp, I'd be going over there. My dental office paperwork was still sitting on the coffee table in her living room.

There was a text message from Melissa when I grabbed my phone off the bed after my shower.

Melissa: Good morning. Or are you back to being afraid of me?

I grinned. This girl knew me way too well. And ironically, just her asking calmed a lot of my fears.

Connor: When can I see you?

Melissa: Give me thirty minutes to not look like a swamp thing.

She could never look like swamp anything, although I had a feeling she put a lot of work into taming those curls every morning. It was almost enough inducement to go over early and find out if I was right. But as a non-stalker, I'd respect her wishes.

Connor: See you in thirty.

I dropped my phone, dressed, brushed my teeth twice, tamed my own hair which had some serious bedhead, and gulped down a small bowl of cereal and milk while my legs fidgeted. Then I brushed my teeth again. Yeah, you could say I was looking forward to seeing her again.

Rob had already left for a yoga retreat in Sedona, so I didn't worry about him catching on to my whereabouts. He was so used to me being gone all the time he hadn't questioned all the nights I'd disappeared this week over to Melissa's place.

I turned on the sprinklers on my way over, adjusting their location so we wouldn't get any boggy spots. It all looked like organized mud right now, but in a few weeks, we'd have a real yard. I could even wave to the neighbors without guilt.

Melissa opened her door and sidled up next to me on the porch, letting our arms brush. My temperature spiked in response, enough to make me want to douse myself with the sprinkler. When she took my hand and led me inside her place, I thought I might spontaneously combust.

She was in a pair of cut-off jean shorts and an old Brad Paisley concert T-shirt. Before I could grab her up and let her know exactly how long thirty minutes felt like, Buster and Sarge charged between us, eager for a group hug.

I bent down and petted their heads. "Hey, guys. Way to play chaperone this morning. Where were you two last night?"

"Regretting it already?" Melissa asked, crossing her arms as she looked at me.

"Not a bit." I held her gaze. *Not. One. Bit.*

"But…" She added.

I sighed. Melissa had this way of digging the truth out of me, even when I couldn't see it for myself. "But we're neighbors. And your granny thinks I'm the crud you scrape off the bottom of your shoe." Her granny also thought Melissa was engaged to her grandson. So did Natalya. Who else was under that impression?

Yeah, I had worries. But Melissa already thought I was a Debby Downer and a Nervous Nellie. I didn't want to escalate that to a Debbie-Relationship-Destroyer and a Never-Come-Over-Again-Nellie by bringing up too much too soon.

Melissa sank into the couch, and I followed, claiming the spot next to her and lacing my fingers with hers. Best feeling ever. Somewhere, an angel got its wings. I was sure of it.

Despite all the reasons to not do this, being with Melissa just felt right.

"I'm ready to talk about Damien."

"Your fiancé?"

"My ex-fiance. Yeah."

"You sure?" I squeezed her hand and she squeezed back.

"I've known for a while he's not in the witness protection program. He only told us that so he could leave with everyone still liking him. And I'm actually kind of glad he's obsessed with his image. Because it would have been a lot easier to leave his dogs at the pound and ditch his granny without a backward glance. Instead, he gave them to me."

I stared at Buster and Sarge at our feet. "These are his dogs?"

"Yeah."

So, the guy was a con artist. And I was a jerk for thinking otherwise. It made sense. Melissa had this big heart, and he'd taken advantage of that. "Did he take money from you?"

Melissa gave a bitter laugh. "No. His family has plenty of money. The place Granny stays in is actually pretty swanky. He didn't need money, he needed freedom. Granny's not the easiest person to get along with, and Buster here has an excitement pee problem. Sarge gets anxious without Buster by his side, so they're a package deal. I think Damien only asked me to marry him so I'd feel more obligated to help out when he left."

"What did he ask you to do?"

"He asked me to keep an eye on Granny and to take care of his dogs until he could come back. And then we'd be together."

Dangling hope like that. What a total piece of garbage. "When did you know it was all a lie?"

Melissa sank deeper into the couch and stared at the ceiling. "He witnessed a kidnapping of a kid whose parents were in a custody battle. Or, I don't know, maybe that part's not even true. But he made it seem like he was in constant contact with the police, and that the kidnapper was part of this criminal ring that involved the dad. And then Damien came to my apartment one morning with his truck packed to the gills. He said they were putting him into protection until the case went to trial, and maybe after that, too. And I believed him. I had no reason not to. My suspicion that it was all made-up built over time, and came to a head when I ran into one of his old girlfriends when I was out jogging. She recognized his dogs."

Melissa turned and hugged me suddenly, taking me by surprise. I relaxed and pulled her closer, kissing her forehead.

"What are you doing?" I whispered.

"Relieving stress." She pulled away reluctantly and smiled. "Am I freaking you out?"

I shook my head. "I'm just going to shut up and listen."

"Good man." She pulled her knees up and hugged them. "He told his ex-girlfriend he was a neurosurgeon and a children's pastor. Oh, and that he had climbed Mount Everest as a birthday gift to himself. And a bunch of other stuff that turned out to be complete lies. We compared enough notes to discount pretty much everything he'd ever told us about himself."

"I told you I was a drug dealer," I blurted out, wishing I'd known the truth about her situation from the beginning. I would have never lied to her, not even as a joke. I saw every conversation we'd ever had in a new light. Why did she even like me?

Melissa turned to study me and rubbed her thumb over the crease in my forehead. "Yeah, but you weren't a convincing liar at all, which I found really attractive." She smiled. "I have to admit, I did, um, check the state dental board records. You are, in fact, a dentist." Her face flamed red, which *I* found really attractive.

The fact that she checked up on me meant she cared. And that meant I couldn't ever keep secrets from her. Not if I wanted to deserve her, and I found I did. "Melissa, I told you I was a drug dealer because... um..." Oh, this was hard. How did I not make myself sound like the world's biggest jerk?

She waited on me, her smile growing brighter with every awkward second that passed. "This ought to be good."

"Okay, it's just that after Natalya, I got sort of jaded. You know, like in the way you wanted to check up on my dental certifications. I assumed that if your fiancé told you he needed to go into the witness protection program... that meant he was..." *Just breathe.* "....a little desperate."

Melissa's eyes widened. "You thought I was the type of woman you had to run away from. Like *Fatal Attraction* level." She stared at me for several seconds, and I wondered if I was about to get slapped. But then she threw back her head and laughed until tears ran down her face. "Oh, dear. I get it now." She wiped a tear away. "You were so afraid of me. Dangerously afraid. Of me."

"So, you're not mad?"

She smiled. "I haven't decided yet. I think Granny's mad enough for the both of us. You have not endeared yourself to me in her eyes. She thought you were sweeping up that grass seed the other night so you could steal it."

"How do I get on her good side? Flowers?"

Melissa shook her head. "She'd find that presumptive."

"Okay. No flowers. Chocolate?"

"Hate, hate, double hate."

"She hates chocolates or she hates cliché gifts?"

"The second one. She'd call you a smarmy butt-kisser for sure."

"Would she use those exact words, though?"

"Yes."

I laughed. Granny was growing on me.

Melissa rubbed my arm. "There's no other way. You'll just have to save my life right in front of her."

"Come again?"

"Yeah, that will work. Clear your schedule for tomorrow night. Do you think your brother and sister would be up for playing villains?"

I had no words and no clue what she was talking about. My

62

mouth opened and closed. Melissa just laughed at my expression and kissed my cheek. "Save the chocolates and flowers for Natalya. She also hates you. But on a positive note, my mom thinks you're cute."

CHAPTER 15

←————————————→

MELISSA

"Granny, I can't seem to ditch this tail." I glanced in my rear view, where Parker was two cars back. I could see Lauren and Clay leaning forward from the back seats. Their grins were obvious, even from this distance. Apparently, summer vacation was a little more boring than they'd anticipated. They'd been happy to join in on my adventure with Granny today.

Granny picked up the set of binoculars on the console between us and turned around to look.

"No, don't." I lowered them from her face. She might have to meet them for real someday, and it would be helpful if she didn't think Connor came from a family of hardened criminals. "We have to act like we don't know they're following us. Best case scenario, we lose them in the next few miles and then circle back to our destination."

"But I could snap a clear picture of them with these bad boys."

She was fascinated with the camera binoculars I'd brought. High-tech spy gear, in her mind. I'd be deleting so many pictures of innocent bystanders off them before returning them to Connor's family. His stepmom used them for bird-watching.

"What happens if we miss the meeting?" Granny asked, glancing at the car's clock. "You said we have to be there at six sharp. That's in ten minutes."

I took a deep breath in. "We'll make it. Leave it to me."

Right on schedule, Parker dropped away from tailing me and drove east towards the field we'd picked as our handoff location. I was giving him a five minute head start to get there. The field was down the road from Sun Valley Heavy Equipment Rental, the business Connor's dad owned.

I made a point of mentioning Sun Valley when we drove past it, and that Connor was there today working with his dad. Granny only harrumphed, but I hoped his nearby location was a detail she'd remember later. Otherwise his rescue would seem all too convenient.

The weeds in the field were overgrown, and a property owner had long ago abandoned rusty farm tools here and there, along with a few old cars that hadn't moved in at least ten years. Basically, it made a pretty great lookout location.

I parked my car behind one of the abandoned trucks and turned to Granny. "Remember, if anyone asks, we're bird-watching. Got it?"

"I got it." Granny picked up the wide brim hat I'd brought her with the fake stuffed birds all over it and stuck it on her head. "You better put yours on, too, Melissa."

I did, smiling to myself. Once we'd involved Connor's stepmom in the planning, she'd come up with details I never would have considered, like these hats. She was on the docket for next week to walk right past us on a busy street and hand off a mystery envelope. She already had a disguise picked out.

I got out and ran around to get Granny's door, helping her into position with her walker and the binoculars. Around the side of the abandoned truck, we had a clear shot to see everything about to go down.

I texted the code word 'birdstalkers' to Connor, Parker, Lauren, and Clay, and set in to wait. Because it was so hot, we had decided to keep lag times to a minimum. The last thing we needed was for Granny to get heatstroke out here while playing spy.

"There they are," I whispered, not thirty seconds later. Parker crept in from the back of the field with a leather briefcase, and Lauren and Clay ducked around a dead farm truck and headed his direction, high stepping through the weeds. All three were sporting white ski masks, sun glasses, and safari hats, and I had to bite back a laugh. They looked like backup dancers in a music video, except without the rhythm.

Granny harrumphed. "These pictures won't help the CIA at all. They could be anyone."

"Our job was just to see how many showed up. Besides, now we know their approximate height and weight. That's something."

"I guess." Granny went back to looking through the binoculars and snapping images.

Parker handed off the briefcase to Clay, shook hands with both him and Lauren, and then my cell phone rang at full volume, right on schedule.

All three slowly turned to look in our direction, and even as part of the plan, their faceless stares still creeped me out.

Granny dropped the binoculars and gripped my arm. "Melissa, your phone."

"I'm trying, I'm trying." I dug my cell out of my back pocket and silenced it while Parker, Clay and Lauren slowly stalked towards us. I'd decided early on with these adventures to never involve weapons, not even fake ones, so they just looked like participants in a cautious game of red light, green light.

I picked up a rock and threw it into the bushes across from us. Two quail let out a warning cry and flew out. The ski masked villains turned to look and froze in their progress.

"Okay, let's go, Granny." I got her in on the passenger side and quickly folded up her walker, shoving it in the back seat. Then I ran around and jumped in, gunning it just enough to give it a sense of urgency, but not so much that my car would bottom out. I pulled onto the street and looked behind us.

Parker, Clay, and Lauren were jumping in Parker's truck and following. They had to be sweating buckets in their costumes. Just my nervousness about pulling this off had turned me into a sweaty mess.

Granny glanced behind us. "Where do we go?"

I tossed her my phone. "Connor's in my list of missed calls. Call him and tell him we're being followed, and we're coming to his dad's office."

"Missed calls?" Granny stared down at my shiny phone like it might be alien tech. She pressed her finger on it cautiously and frowned when it didn't do whatever she was expecting. She pressed on it again and again until Siri boomed out, "I don't understand."

Granny stared at the phone. "Me either. Who is this?"

The phone didn't answer, which really ticked her off. I grabbed it out of her hand before she could bang it on the glove box. So much for that part of the plan. Hopefully, Granny wouldn't be suspicious of Connor showing up like a genie the second we pulled in. Which was in about thirty seconds. At the end of the street, I turned into the Sun Valley Heavy Equipment parking lot and scrolled down to Connor's name, pressing send.

He answered on the first ring. "Melissa?"

"Hey, we need help. Some bad guys are following us. We've just pulled into your parking lot."

I hung up and turned to Granny. "He'll be here in a minute."

Parker drove up next to us, and Clay and Lauren got out to circle our car.

I hit the lock button. "You okay, Granny?"

She glanced at the two circling and balled her fists. "It takes a lot to scare me."

That's what I was afraid of. This adventure would be a lot to one-up. Spotting Connor sprinting towards us filled me with complete relief. This meant the end of our adventure. He yelled at Clay and Lauren, pretended to get in a fist fight with Clay, and then ran them off back to Parker's truck. After they took off down the road, I hit the unlock button and jumped out.

"Thank you." I went to hug Connor and bumped him with my bird hat instead. He pulled it off my head and smoothed back my curls, probably catching a bit of sweat that was beading off my forehead.

"I'm so gross," I murmured.

"Not gross." He was so going to kiss me. I knew it. I was anticipating it.

"You two forgotten I exist over here?" I turned to see Granny leaning out of the car, looking quite irritated. Not because we'd been threatened by faceless bad guys, but because Connor was paying attention to me. And in that moment, I knew it wouldn't matter if Connor pulled me out of a burning building. He wasn't going to win her over because he wasn't Damien.

I'd just have to keep them apart from now on. Connor didn't deserve to be held against a standard that didn't exist. He didn't have to win her over, or Natalya over. My relationship with him could just be mine, and mine alone.

CHAPTER 16

← ⸻ →

CONNOR

Melissa was going to be the death of me. I couldn't imagine a day without her in it, and knew she felt the same way about me, but no one in her life was allowed to know. Not Natalya, not Granny, not her parents, not even the mailman. The mail truck had pulled up one day while we were out watering the grass together, and she'd dropped my hand like a hot potato and pretended I didn't exist until it drove off. I also hadn't missed the way she'd angled her stack of mail away from me so I couldn't see it.

That was what led me here, to this Monday afternoon, a month after the stupid car chase that ended with Granny giving me the cold shoulder. Melissa was in her bathroom freshening up after work, and I was staring at the stack of mail on her counter.

Okay, staring is not quite accurate. I was also sifting through it. But that was it. I wasn't going to open anything, not even the letter on the bottom of the stack addressed to *The Beautiful Melissa Cooke*. It had no return address, but I didn't need three guesses to know who it was from.

Damien was like toxic mold—under the surface, eating away at the foundation of our relationship. I needed an expert to find out the extent of the damage. Unfortunately, I was dating the expert, and the thought of asking her to get rid of his influence had my insides twisting.

The bathroom door opened down the hall, and the mail jumped out of my hands and fell all over the floor. I was such an idiot. I scooped it up as fast as I could, just in time to be holding it all when she walked out and stared at me.

"What are you doing?" She grinned at my panicked face, but then realizing what I was holding, she cleared her expression to something neutral and took it out my hands. Walking over to the recycle can, she sorted and dropped the junk mail into it. I noticed the letter from Damien was included in the junk mail, though she didn't rip it in half like the credit card offers. Did that mean she would fish it out later after I left?

I couldn't take it anymore. The not talking about it. The not knowing.

"Was that a letter from Damien?"

She froze. "Yes. I don't write him back and I haven't opened one in months. He sends Granny's letters to me, too. Like he's afraid I wouldn't go see her unless he gave me a reason."

"You should tell Granny the truth."

"No." Her answer was immediate and firm, and I almost backed off. But I had to know why.

"She can take it."

"She can't. He's all she has. Her son pays for her care, but he won't visit. No one will visit. It's just me and Damien's letters. If I tell her, she won't even have that."

"You don't know that. Maybe she'd write and talk some sense into him."

Melissa whirled on me. "And then what? He comes home and takes his dogs back? I like my life the way it is. I don't want him to know I know. I don't want anything to change. Yeah, my life is hard, but it's *my* hard. It's manageable." She stared at me, looking ashamed, but also determined.

"You won't even change it to include me?"

The pause after was like a bullet to my heart.

"Not right now."

But what she meant was no, she wouldn't change it. I took in a deep breath. I needed to leave. This felt final, and I wasn't ready to beg when Melissa couldn't even see what I was asking for. "I should go home and get some things done. I'll see you later."

She followed me to the door. "Connor, wait."

I turned to look at her, but after several painful seconds, it was obvious she didn't have anything to offer me except her regret, the kind of regret that came with wishing we could keep things just the way they were. So I left.

CHAPTER 17

←————————————→

MELISSA

The grass was nice and thick now. Thick enough for me to sit on it while the sprinkler soaked me. This was usually the time Connor came over and made dinner with me, but we hadn't done that in a week, and I couldn't go inside and face that yet. I'd been sitting here for ten minutes, trying to figure out how to fix the mess that was my life while a sprinkler pegged me in the back of the head. Buster and Sarge watched me from the other side of the lawn, their expressions not necessarily judgmental, but a little concerned. Some women eat cookies when they're sad. Me? I was okay with staying right here until I felt better.

What exactly was I supposed to say to Granny? I didn't have proof Damien wasn't in the witness protection program. I could hire an investigator, I supposed. Get photographic evidence. But I didn't have the money for that, nor did I have money to take Damien to court if he decided to come back and take his dogs.

Of course, he could do that whether I kept up his lie or not. He could stop writing Granny at any point, for any reason. I had been loyal to him in every way possible, both when we were together, and every moment since. Mostly out of fear.

And the one guy who had deserved my loyalty? I'd ditched him at the first sign of pushback. Connor was probably watching me out his window and patting himself on the back that he'd dodged this bullet.

My neighbor across the street came outside to move her garbage can. I waved, letting her know I was fine. I was so not fine.

"Everything okay?" she called out.

"Yep. Just cooling off." I jumped to my feet, finally motivated to move by sheer embarrassment. I couldn't stay in limbo anymore. Not in this yard, not in life.

After getting the dogs fed and taking a quick shower, I called up Natalya first. She'd been a casualty of all the things I'd been avoiding lately, and I owed her an apology.

"Melissa?"

She sounded so surprised to hear from me that I burst into tears.

"I've been a bad friend."

"You have. But I figured something big was going on, and when you were ready, you'd tell me about it."

"When did you get so wise? There is something going on, and I do want to tell you about it."

"Flattery is a good tactic, Melissa. But I'm still mad at you."

"I'm sorry."

"I know. Should I come over?"

"Yes, please. This is definitely a face-to-face kind of conversation." Buster and Sarge would be thrilled to see her. And I needed a friend. Except, maybe breaking the news about Connor with him right next door was a bad idea. "Nat, I should probably tell you what it is first. You might not want to come over once you know."

"Melissa, I already know. I knew the second you started making excuses about hanging out that you were dating Connor. I just hoped I was wrong. But I'm not wrong, am I?"

"No, you're not wrong."

"You sound sad. Did Connor break your heart? Already? I'll break his knee caps."

"What? No. No breaking anything. I'm not sad about Connor. Okay, I am sad about him, but we'll get to that. There's something else I have to tell you. It's about Damien."

"Did you write and tell him it's over? The poor man. But you can't feel guilty for moving on. It was inevitable with your situation."

"Damien's not in the witness protection program." I ripped it off like a Band-Aid, not wanting Natalya to sympathize with my fake plight a second longer. "He only told me that so I'd take the dogs and Granny when he left."

There was a long pause. A really long pause.

"Nat?"

"I'm coming over. See you in five." She ended the call.

True to her word, she came straight over and wrapped me in a big hug the second I opened the door. I was so relieved. Because the Damien thing was an even bigger secret. An older one. And if it had been me, I would have been really hurt.

I hugged her tighter. "I should have told you Damien was a huge liar the second I knew."

Natalya nodded against my shoulder. Then she pulled away, keeping ahold of my arms. Buster took that as an invitation to squeeze between us and beg for love. Natalya patted his fur before shaking her head at me. "We sure pick 'em, Melissa."

"Right?" I wiped at a tear threatening to fall.

"Just tell me everything now. And then all is forgiven. I promise." Natalya picked up Buster and headed to the couch.

So, I did. I told her everything about Damien, and my growing feelings for Connor, and how he said I should tell Granny the truth about her grandson. I told her what my response had been to that suggestion, which sounded even more horrible in retelling. Natalya didn't interrupt or offer advice. She just listened, occasionally biting her nail. It was her one beauty vice.

"I don't want to break the news to Granny. But he's right. I have to. I have to tell everyone, no matter how humiliating it all is."

"Do you want me to come with you when you tell Granny?" Natalya asked.

I thought about it. Part of me wanted to say yes, but while it would make me feel better to have her there, it wouldn't help Granny. "No, I'll go. Thank you, Nat. For everything."

I glanced at the clock. I had an hour before visiting hours were over. Normally on Tuesday nights, Granny was watching her recording of *The Beautiful and Reckless*, which they taped for her during her lunch hour when everyone else wanted to watch the Game Show Network. But I was pretty sure the soap opera's season was over, and it was on reruns.

Either way, if I waited another day I'd find more reasons to put it off. Natalya agreed. She gave me a parting hug and a push out the door.

I called the retirement center on the way and told them to notify Granny I'd be there in ten minutes.

I'd brought along Damien's letters to me before heading out the door, including the letter I'd fished out of the recycle can after Connor confronted me about it. As many times as I'd considered burning the whole pile, something always held me back. Why?

Well, because I had no idea what to do with them. Just like I had no idea what to tell Granny. While I drove, my mind hit dead end after dead end. Nothing I considered saying to Granny seemed right. Nothing would make this all okay.

When I showed my I.D. inside and was escorted down to Granny's room, she was waiting for me by the window, looking out on the garden where hummingbirds often zipped back and forth, visiting flowers. Of course, Granny's gaze wasn't trained on the hummingbirds. She was watching two construction workers repairing the sidewalk on the other side of the breezeway.

"Tabitha has been in and out of her door, offering them cold drinks and asking questions." Granny said in greeting. "Pestering those two handsome young things. Ridiculous for someone her age."

"Mmm, hmm. Very ridiculous." As was this pot calling the kettle black.

She turned to me and spotted the stack of letters in my hands. "What are those?"

I came closer. "Damien's letters to me."

She reached out, and I let her take the one off the top. "But they're mostly unopened." She slid her finger across the flap, and I didn't try to stop her.

"What does it say?" I asked.

She read it herself for almost a minute before dropping the letter on the little round table in front of her and looking up at me. "He says that he misses you and can't say anything about where he's living or what he's doing. And then he tells you some marvelous stories about where he's living and what he's doing." She smiled and was quiet for a long time, which was very unlike her.

"Granny, I have to tell you something."

She wrung her hands together and then shoved them in her lap. "Go ahead and say it."

Did she know? The unease I sensed in her body language made saying it aloud that much harder.

"I don't think..." I took a deep breath. "I don't think Damien left because he had to. I think he left on purpose. I think he's lying to us."

Granny's mouth trembled. "I'm so sorry, my girl." She reached out and grasped my hands with her cold, thin ones. Her skin was so soft and fragile.

"Don't be sorry. I'm fine. I'm just worried about you."

She shook her head. "I've known. I've known for a while. But I thought you believed it, and as long as that was the case, I didn't want to be the one to break your heart. That was selfish of me."

I dropped into the chair across from her, stunned and relieved all at once. "Then I'm just as selfish because I've been doing the same thing. I thought I was protecting you from the truth. But now we know."

"Now we know," she repeated. "I *was* being selfish, though. I could have told him off months ago, but I liked getting his letters. Still do. He's a more attentive letter writer than he ever was a visitor."

"Then we let him write," I said with a nod. We'd keep things just as they were, though the thought didn't quite comfort me the way it used to.

"What is it?" Granny asked, reading the discomfort in my face.

"What if he comes back? He could take the dogs away from me."

"Damien's not going to do anything of the sort. You'll keep those dogs as long as I live. And after I'm gone my money will allow you to bribe him or sue him or whatever tickles your fancy."

"Granny, I can't take your money."

"Not take, inherit. Now don't get your panties in a twist. You don't get all of it. Just enough to really tick off everyone else."

It was useless to argue, so I gave it up. Granny had a great lawyer. I'm sure she had all sorts of fun ideas about how to cause drama on her way out. Iron clad drama. The thought made me smile.

Granny's eyes narrowed. "You've fallen for someone else, haven't you? That's why you came to clear the air, so to speak."

"No." The lie slipped out automatically, but I couldn't let it go uncorrected. "Okay, maybe."

"Is it Connor? He gives you a pretty yard and some sweet talk, and bam," Granny smacked the table. "He's taken you in. Just like Damien."

"He's not like Damien, Granny."

"Well, good." She nodded. "That's good."

It was weird to adjust my thinking so drastically. Granny hadn't hated Connor because he wasn't Damien. She'd feared he might be just like him. I took a deep breath, knowing if I could be successfully honest in this and survive, I might as well be honest in everything. "Granny, those adventures we go on—"

Granny stuck her hands over her ears and shook her head. "I can't hear you. I can't hear you."

"Granny!" I frowned at her until she stopped.

"Melissa, let an old woman have a little fun in life. Honestly!" And then she smiled and told me to turn on the T.V. so we could watch the news together.

CHAPTER 18

CONNOR

My life was so dull without Melissa in it. Work was a good distraction during the day. I had new patients I was working to build a rapport with, and a new team at the office helping me learn the ropes.

But I had no one to talk to about it at the end of the day. Rob was usually playing the bongos while I made dinner for myself, by myself. Watching T.V. alone in my room only reinforced how much I missed hanging out with Melissa. It wasn't that I didn't have other friends, but I didn't ache to be with them the way that I ached to be with her.

But obviously, she didn't feel the same way. And I was too much of a chicken to make sure I was right about that.

Rob's shadow in my doorway pulled me from my T.V. trance. What was I watching? Oh, yeah, an infomercial for a rotisserie grill. If the grill came with a chef to make all the food, I was so in.

"What's up, Rob?"

"I think you should check on our neighbor."

"Melissa?" My voice cracked on her name, and I cleared my throat. It probably wasn't her. We had lots of neighbors.

"Yeah, Melissa. The bongo hater. She was sitting in the middle of the yard, getting tagged in the back of the head with the sprinkler, over and over again. Like a zombie. It was freaking me out. Maybe take a baseball bat with you."

"You want me to show up at her door with a baseball bat?" Rob considered this for several seconds. "Well, I would."

"When was this?" I asked.

"I don't know. Like, at five-thirty? I watched until I got a phone call, and when I came back to the window she was gone."

"Okay, I'll think about it." My fear of showing up uninvited was a lot stronger now that I knew what I had to lose if she didn't want me there. But my worry for her outweighed my fears, so I got up and slid on a pair of shoes.

"That was some fast thinking," Rob called out to me as I headed out the door. Without a baseball bat, I might add.

I could see Melissa's car wasn't there, but I still knocked on her door just to make sure. Sarge and Buster barked at me, but there was no answer. This was stupid. She was probably fine. What did Rob know, anyway? It was a hot day today. Maybe she'd just wanted to cool off. She was fine without me.

I sighed and turned to slide down and sit on her doormat. It wasn't like I could get more unhappy than I already was. Not by talking to her and seeing if she was okay.

Sitting in the growing dark with just the sound of lazy crickets and an occasional hoot of an owl gave me some time to think. I'd been so concerned about my own happiness that I hadn't bothered to worry about what made Melissa happy.

Here she was, taking care of Granny and Damien's dogs. Not with resentment, but with fierce love. And I'd asked her to risk all that for me. What had I offered her besides the pleasure of my company? Who was the person taking care of Melissa while she was taking care of everything else? Who was looking out for her interests? Fiercely loving *her*?

I wanted it to be me. And I hadn't told her that. I dropped my head in my hands, letting the guilt wash over me. The guilt felt good, necessary and useful, like the way my body reacted after a hard workout. Apparently, my conscience had been overdue for a good workout, too.

I thought about all the things I might say to her, but when the light from Melissa's headlights hit me ten minutes later as she turned into the carport, my stomach gave a kick of fear.

"Hey," I called out when she started walking up. I didn't want to scare her to death.

"Connor?"

I stood when she approached, feeling dumb for waiting on her doorstep when I could have just watched for her from my house.

"Wanna come in?" she asked.

"Yeah, that'd be great." I moved aside for her to unlock the door. She flipped on the porch light and nudged Buster and Sarge out of the way so I could squeeze inside before getting mauled.

I bent down and rubbed Sarge's big ol' head. "Hey guy, I've missed you this week." I hadn't considered how Melissa might take that until I looked up and saw her watching us. Had she missed me, too?

She ducked her head and walked toward the kitchen. "I haven't eaten dinner. Do you mind if I warm something up?"

"I'll help you." I knew she liked those tiny rectangle frozen dinners, and usually paired it with a side salad if she wasn't too tired to throw one together. While she microwaved her meal, I washed my hands and then got out a head of lettuce and a few other vegetables from the fridge and got to chopping.

Neither of us said anything for the longest time, but it wasn't awkward. It was more like we were getting reacquainted with being in each other's space and we didn't want to ruin it with attempts at conversation.

I placed Melissa's salad on the table with silverware and a napkin and went to sit on the couch, where I could lean over the back and see her without being in the way while she ate.

"Wait, you aren't going to eat anything?" She looked down at the salad I'd made her and then at the clean counters now that I'd put everything away.

"I already ate. But don't worry about me." I was worried enough for both of us. I couldn't exactly confess my love to her while she ate Salisbury steak and potatoes out of a plastic container. But my brain couldn't do small talk right now either.

I got up and walked around Melissa's living room, stopping at her bookshelf where I saw the thick pink manuscript shelved along with some actual novels. "Will Granny kill me if I keep reading this?" I asked, sliding the manuscript out and holding it up for Melissa to see.

"Go right ahead. I think she was secretly pleased you liked it."

"Enough to thaw her cold heart?"

Melissa laughed. "Eventually."

I settled back into the couch to read, though it wasn't as much fun without an angry Melissa looming over me, demanding I hand it back. I knew that day she'd be all sorts of wonderful trouble; I'd just had no idea how much.

At the point where the mafia's number-one informant had decided to risk it all for love, Melissa slipped onto the couch next to me and leaned in. How much time had gone by? Five minutes? Fifty? She'd changed into pajamas. She'd also brushed her teeth. I knew because her warm, minty breath hit my ear, and the words on the page swam together until I couldn't remember a single detail of it.

"Connor, I want to fit you in my life."

I placed the manuscript on the table and turned to pull her into my arms with her face snuggled in against my neck. My whole body relaxed for the first time in a week. Her closeness had become essential to me, and it took almost losing her to figure that out.

"I want to be in your life. But it wasn't my place to set the terms. I'm sorry."

"Don't be sorry. Just don't rub it in when I say you were right."

"I was right?"

She lightly slugged me in the ribs. "See, you're already rubbing it in."

"I'm not. I promise."

"Well, actually, it's okay if you are. I told Natalya and Granny about Damien. And I feel so much better. I was being loyal to someone who didn't deserve my loyalty, and by doing so, damaging my relationships with all the people who matter the most. You showed me that."

I pulled back just enough to be able to look her in the eyes. "You're amazing, you know that? And I realized something, too. I want to be your person."

"My person?" She cocked her head.

"Well, I was going to say hero, but that's a little too Enrique Iglesias for me."

She laughed. "*I Wanna Be Your Hero* is a Def Leppard song. And yeah, you can be my hero whenever you want, Connor. Like maybe next week? When Granny and I start to decode a secret message left under a park bench and a masked man snatches it out of my hands?" She put her palms together in a plea, begging me with her big, brown eyes.

"Yeah, alright." I'd do anything for her, and she knew it. "But what I meant before I unintentionally quoted Enrique Iglesias—"

"And Def Leppard," she added with a smile.

"—Was that you do all these nice things for everyone else, and I want to be the person who does nice things for you."

Melissa bit her lip. "What kinds of nice things?" She leaned forward until she was absolutely teasing me with her mouth so close to mine.

"Anything you'd like." I closed the distance and did my best to show her all the nice things I had in store for her. I was nothing if not the most giving and attentive neighbor she'd ever have. I'd make sure of it.

EPILOGUE — ONE YEAR LATER

CONNOR

I took in a deep breath and gazed up at the grassy hill ahead of us, where fifteen umbrellas with letters taped on the back spelled out the most important question I ever planned to ask.

Today was going to be epic.

"Quit daydreaming and pay attention, Connor!" Granny swiped the walkie-talkie out of my hand and held down the talk button. "Whoever is holding the Y in MARRY better stop twirling that thing this instant! I can see you through these binoculars, little blonde girl!"

Maybe today would be epic as in an epic disaster. With Granny, you never knew. I was regretting a lot of things when it came to including her in all this—letting her supervise, teaching her how the buttons on a walkie-talkie worked, and dropping my guard enough for her to first steal the binoculars out of my hands and then the walkie-talkie. I was never getting either of them back. A tug-o-war with an octogenarian at a public park wasn't exactly on my list of things to do today.

"The line looks good, Granny. Don't worry, Melissa will love it."

Granny turned and glared at me. "One little slip up with those children you hired, and it might say, 'WILL YOU ARM ME?' or 'ILL YOU ARE.'" Granny put the binoculars up to her eyes again. "'YOU WILL MARRY ME.' That one would really knock her socks off. There's nothing a woman loves more than an ultimatum."

"First of all, there is no child labor involved in this proposal. Everyone volunteered to be here because they love Melissa. And second of all, nobody has swapped any words around. They're just excited and a little twirly." I had underestimated how much kids liked to spin umbrellas, although an upside-down letter wouldn't be the end of the world. The neighbor kids and their parents had been ecstatic at the idea of helping me pull this surprise off. After all, they'd been there the day I met Melissa. Surprise birthday party, surprise proposal. Why not?

Not that popping the question would be a surprise. Melissa and I had talked about marriage a lot. I was getting very familiar with her wedding Pinterest board, and the thing was growing by the day. But despite that, I wanted the moment when I dropped to one knee and gave her the ring in my shirt pocket to be more than a casual gesture. I wanted to wow her.

My phone pinged and I pulled it out of my pocket to read the text from Natalya. Almost there.

My stomach gave a kick of excitement. This was it.

MELISSA

Everyone was acting weird today. Connor's head had been somewhere else this morning when I stopped by his place. We had a good time making waffles and eating breakfast together, but he'd been antsy, and when I asked if he was interested in going to the park with us later, he'd declined. Maybe he was just trying to give Natalya and me some girl time. He *had* given me a particularly nice send off, kissing me like he might not ever see me again and whispering how much he loved me.

But then, Natalya had acted strange too. She showed up dressed like it was prom night, and thanks to her last minute makeover, now I was too, although I'd drawn the line at wearing heels. My rose-colored sneakers matched this dress better anyway.

She currently had a death grip on the steering wheel which was in complete opposition to the goofy smile on her face.

"Okay, what is going on, Natalya? Why couldn't we bring the dogs to the park? And why are we dressed like this? Is there some hot jogger you're hoping to run into or something?"

Natalya gave a high-pitched laugh. "Well, wouldn't that be nice, but no, I'm not counting on any hot jogger action. And as much as I love Buster and Sarge, they jump on people too much so they can't come today. I'm lucky my dress survived as it is, just walking into your house."

"What people?" This particular park wasn't busy, and I was always careful to keep them away from everyone else out walking their dogs.

"You'll see in a minute." Natalya pulled into the parking lot of the park and turned to grin at me. "I have a blindfold for you. Don't freak out."

A normal person would freak out. But that news actually made everything that much less weird. "Oh, this is a Granny thing." I should have known, although I didn't know why I wasn't in on planning this adventure. Maybe they wanted my reactions to be genuine. I was probably about to be stuffed in a trunk or pulled into a van or something. Granny was going to love this.

Natalya came around to the passenger side and put the bandana blindfold around my head, careful to keep it from tugging at my hair as she tied a knot in the back. "Okay, I'm going to take your hand and lead you. Just walk, friend. I think you were right to say no to heels today."

"Am I supposed to act scared or confused?" I asked. I gripped her hand harder as we slowed to step up onto the curb. I did not want to fall and have a wardrobe malfunction. This dress showed off my legs, but that was all I wanted to show off in public. "Am I a rich socialite being kidnapped for money?"

Natalya laughed. "Oh, honey. You pretend to be anything you'd like for the next few minutes."

"Well, that's vague." I hoped this wasn't going to be so over the top that we had the cops called on us. A trip down to the police department was not my idea of a relaxing afternoon.

We slowed, and from my other side, an arm went around my shoulder. "What did you tell her, Nat?"

"Mom?" I turned my head towards her voice. "Are you in on this, too?"

"Yep. Dad's here too."

"Hi, honey." Dad's deep voice came from right behind me.

"Hi, Dad. Who else is here?"

"You'll see in a minute," Natalya answered for him. "We have about ten more steps."

We walked a little farther across the grass and then stopped.

"Positions! Everyone get in position!" That voice was definitely Granny's. Maybe she had decided to turn the tables on me, and she was now the one planning the spy adventures while I was just along for the ride. It figured.

"Granny, am I being kidnapped?"

Granny cackled. "In a matter of speaking. The romance is overwhelming me, Connor, my boy. Good luck with this."

"Connor?" I turned my head back and forth even though I couldn't see anything but red cloth. Was Connor here, too?

His warm hand took mine. I recognized the callouses on his fingertips, the temperature of his palms, and the familiar way he laced his fingers with mine. "I'm right here, Melissa. I have a question for you."

I took in a deep breath and let it out. Okay, now things made sense. Much more than fake kidnappings or scoping out the park for Natalya's next boyfriend. A peace settled over me. This wasn't a surprising turn of events, just a surprising way of making it official.

Connor kissed the tips of my fingers. I ran my hand across his jaw. I could tell he was smiling. It made me smile, too. Dang, I loved this man.

"Ready for the blindfold to come off?" he asked.

"Yep."

"Just look right at me when I take it off, okay?" His hands slid behind my head and undid the knot before pulling the bandana away. I looked up at him and blinked at the sudden change in light while he smoothed my hair. Then I watched him pull a little black velvet box out of his shirt pocket and drop to one knee.

I was so intent on his smile and the most perfect sparkly ring winking at me in the sun, that it took several seconds before I realized there was a line of kids holding umbrellas that spelled out WILL YOU MARRY ME? up on the hill behind him. Some of the letters were dancing. It was the most adorable thing I'd ever seen. He'd done all this for me?

Connor turned and gestured to the umbrellas. "Melissa, will you marry me?"

I laughed and reached down to hug him. "Yeah, I totally will."

Granny's trusty Kodak camera began to click as Connor slipped the ring on my finger. It was a perfect fit. Just like him.

The End

Thank you, lovely readers. Reviews are much appreciated. If you enjoyed Connor and Melissa's story, don't miss the next two full-length novels in the series, I Hated You First (about Lauren and Denver) and Carpool Crush (Jenny and Noah). All my author links are here: https://linktr.ee/rjohn

Other titles by Rachel John:

Engaging Mr. Darcy
Emma the Matchmaker
Persuading the Captain
Dashing into Disaster

An Unlikely Alliance
Her Charming Distraction
Protector of Her Heart
Pretending He's Mine

Matchmaker for Hire
Bethany's New Reality
Gorgeous and the Geek

The Stand-in Christmas Date
The Christmas Bachelor Auction
The Christmas Wedding Planners
The Accidental Christmas Match Up

ABOUT THE AUTHOR

Rachel John lives in Arizona with her husband and four kids. Besides hanging out with the characters in her head, she likes to jam out to music that annoys her kids, read romance books, occasionally go running as part of her zombie apocalypse prepping, and work on family history. She has a fairly useless English Literature degree from Arizona State University but learned the most about writing and craft from the awesome writer community online. Rachel is most active on Instagram with the handle @racheljohnwrites. Come say hi!

Printed in Great Britain
by Amazon

83174836R00058